Sherlock Holmes and John Watson:

The Night They Met

19 Ways the World's Most Legendary
Love Story Might Have Begun

By

Atlin Merrick

Paperback ISBN 978-0-9935136-0-2
ePub ISBN 978-0-9935136-1-9

Published in the UK by Improbable Press Limited
71-75 Shelton Street, Covent Garden, London, WC2H 9JQ
Cover design by www.staunch.com

For

Arthur Conan Doyle & Joseph Merrick

and

for my family, with love

Eventually, soulmates meet,
for they have the same hiding place.

-Robert Brault

"Dr. Watson, Mr. Sherlock Holmes,"
said Stamford, introducing us.

-Arthur Conan Doyle

Table of Contents

Time Immemorial

Waterloo Train Station, London—1931

They sat on the bench and they held hands.

They watched the pigeons.

They watched the scalloped arms on the four-faced clock go round awhile.

"Do you wonder about time?" asked the one.

The other gazed at two birds nuzzling atop the clock. It took him awhile to stop wondering, but when he did he answered the boy beside him. "Sometimes," he said, "Sometimes mummy says there's not enough."

Five-year-old John Watson shifted his bum on the bench. The bench was hard and uncomfortable and his legs jutted out in front of him like pale little sticks. "No, I mean clocks and things."

Four-year-old Sherlock Holmes followed his new friend's gaze to the dials on the station clock across from them. It was really four clocks, one facing in each of the cardinal directions. Sherlock blinked at the thing and thought. When he was done thinking he said, "No," and then scootched on the bench, too. Though Sherlock's legs were a bit longer than John's, they too were not long enough. It would be better if they weren't sitting, Sherlock thought, so he said, "Let's go look."

Together the children wriggled their way off the black station bench, never letting go of one another's hand. Once their feet made landfall Sherlock Holmes politely waited while John Watson hitched up too-big trousers with one small fist. "Stevie gave 'em to me," John said by way of explanation. Sherlock deduced, though he wouldn't know that word for half a dozen years yet, that Stevie was an older family relation, very tidy, right-handed like John, and had often carried an old watch in his pocket.

"Daddy says they'll fit me quick as blinks," John explained further. At the time he'd said this, John's daddy had frowned. Though neither boy knew it, John's father was like Sherlock's mummy; always thinking there wasn't enough time and so spending far too much of it worrying.

At last well-situated, John nodded. Two little boys, lost in Waterloo station not quite near midnight, held tight to one another and walked through the station until they were standing directly under the great black-white-gold clock. They each imagined they could hear it ticking and maybe they did but only for a second. As soon as they were beneath the grand thing Sherlock backed up a bit, for he had a four-year-old's justified fear that big things can fall on little heads. Because he had John's hand in his, John stepped with him and it was all just as well because as soon as they shifted one of the pigeons on top of the clock relieved herself, right where the boys had been.

Despite being alone together in one of the biggest train stations in all of London, poop did what poop does: Tickled the human funny bone beyond all sensible sense. Both boys fell into such a fit of giggles that they ended collapsing where they stood.

Wheezy with mirth and tired from the late hour, they splayed their legs out in front of them, looked up at the clock, and discussed important things.

"My great-grandmum said they didn't used to have the same time all over. Did you know that?"

Sherlock was watching the pigeons again. He liked looking at busy things because he wanted to figure out what they were thinking. "Nope," he said, shifting 'til his shoulder pressed at John's and the side of his hand rested against the side of John's hand. There. Now he felt not so lost.

John wiggled his feet in that fitful way of the energetic, tapping the side of Sherlock's foot over and over, a soothing metronome. "Gran said that every place had its own time for a long, long time and then the teregraff came along and changed all those things, she says."

Sherlock frowned this thought deep into his head and then had a bright idea. "Maybe," he piped up, "that's why there are four clocks. Because there used to be more times!"

John gasped. This sounded very smart. "You're very smart," he said with the deepest admiration.

Sherlock grinned a big, gap-toothed grin.

They wiggled because they were four and five and a little over-tired in the way that makes you a bit hyper, their shoulders tap-tap-tapping against each other in a steady rhythm, and after awhile Sherlock asked, "Where are you going?"

John opened his eyes. He'd been trying to listen to the clock but he was pretty sure it didn't really tick so loud they could hear it. Though maybe it did. If he listened close.

"To the seashore to get sunburnt."

Sherlock nodded because clearly that's why everyone came to Waterloo station. "Me too."

John was about to ask Sherlock if he collected the prettiest rocks from the beach but right then another pigeon pooped. The boys were in such a fit of hysteria that they didn't at first hear when a man shouted, hysterical, "Johnny!"

And then John's daddy was scooping him off the floor and Sherlock was standing up and clasping his hands behind his back, very suddenly trying not to cry, because his brain might be only little but it was a very smart brain and he knew John was going to go away now and he would be lost all by himself.

While John's daddy squeezed him, John's mummy bent down and looked into Sherlock's eyes. "Where are your parents?" she asked gently.

In the end John's parents helped Sherlock find his parents and in the end the boys waved goodbye, each of them off for an Easter holiday at the shore, though their destinations were miles and miles from one another and so there was no way they could play.

*

John Watson was a smart boy, too, and smart boys can find the address of other boys if they get the help of grown-ups.

The funny thing is, by the time John's letter found Sherlock, Sherlock's letter had found John.

Though they were just small, each boy had much to say in his notes to the other, and along with talking about pigeons and clocks and the beach and ice cream and candy floss and rocks, they made a plan to meet at Waterloo station next Easter, when both their families went again on holiday.

Their plan failed.

Mostly because Sherlock's brother Mycroft got sick, so the entire family had to wait an extra day before going to the shore. Sherlock hated Mycroft every minute of that particular trip, he hated every grain of sand on that beach, and he did his best to make sure everyone knew just how hard he could hate things—very! He also wrote John eight letters during those four days and said in the high, strident tones of insufferable five-year-olds everywhere, "You best post these when we get back!"

Needless to say young Master Holmes learned quick-smart not to speak to his mother in this way. Only once there had been an apology (in writing), did mummy agree to post Sherlock's correspondence to his friend.

And so it went. The boys wrote letters over that next year. The talk was of clocks still, and birds, favourite books, the absolute badness of finding worms in your apple, and again they made their plan to find one another underneath the clock.

This time they succeeded.

"You're big!" shouted Sherlock to seven-year-old John, who had indeed grown. "So's your hair!" said John back, pushing short fingers into his friend's messy mop. They sat on their bench, held hands, and talked the hour swift away.

And so it went, once a year for nearly a dozen years. In between times the boys wrote. They sent one another small gifts. John's were usually things he'd found, Sherlock's things he'd made. Then, come the beginning of the long Easter weekend, two boys and two sets of patient parents met for an hour underneath the four-faced clock in Waterloo train station. The boys would chatter fast about the year just past and the one coming, the parents would keep a close eye on the time, and before the boys knew it they were off to separate holidays.

By 1941 the tone of their letters changed, each note wistful with *what ifs*...each letter full of words not quite said yet somehow still there on the page, as if the ghostly remnants of an erasure.

In 1943 things changed again. John Watson went not to war, for he was still too young, but to medical school. That and a job did away with leisure time and holidays and for the next year John succeeded in writing Sherlock only once, replying to Sherlock's long letter about university, then John didn't reply to the second because he wasn't there to receive it.

By this time Sherlock was an experimental man, stealing hours between classes in any lab that would have him. He mixed and measured things, tested, burned, soaked, and stirred, and during these years Sherlock Holmes fell in love with chemistry, its formulaic certainty, its catalysing surprises. He loved puzzles too, and with the vaguest of clues could figure out who'd stolen morphine from the dean's son, the one who'd come back from war without his legs, or which student was sending threatening messages to a strict-grading tutor. Sherlock knew also that the difficult, esoteric work he did with both his chemistry and biology professors was why no one prodded him to sign up, but about that Sherlock didn't care.

What he did care about was something he learnt a year after it happened: John Watson had joined the army.

"What do you mean you can't find him?" Sherlock shouted at the desk clerk. "John H. Watson. Watson, John H." Sherlock waved a letter, "I need to send this to him! I think he was in France!"

It didn't matter how many times he spelled the name or how strident his voice went, Sherlock never got to send his letter. Mostly because John Watson was nowhere near France.

On the suspicion that the Afghan Shah was again about to wander from his promised neutrality, seeking support *from* and supplying support *to* Germany, British soldiers, including

11

John, had been sent to Kabul. Though in the end Afghanistan remained impartial, not so some of its people.

John Watson was invalided home, an Afghan bullet hole in his shoulder, his fledging surgeons career over before it'd barely begun.

Unknowing of all of this, Sherlock tried for six months to send his letter.

He carried it in his pocket. It became a talisman. He stopped in every recruitment office he found and asked carefully, because by now Sherlock knew the entire world was dim as dirt. "W.a.t.s.o.n. Watson. John H. I need to send a letter."

By the time Sherlock finally found where John was, John's letter found him.

...will be in London for Easter I think, the letter concluded, *shall we meet under the clock?*

Sherlock read John's two page letter twelve times. He found that letter a puzzle, and he was exceedingly good at those. Each reading he found a new puzzle piece. A word badly written, a phrase left out where a phrase ought to be. A tone ringing false or one too true. In the end Sherlock Holmes tore up his talisman and he wrote a new letter to John.

...Easter, yes please, it concluded.

And then concluded again. *Yes.*

And again. *Yes.*

And again.

Yes.

*

The air buzzed with the anticipation of years.

That was the poetical way to put it, John mused, straightening his tie. If asked for something with a more earthy spin, John would say the April air was blood-warm with need and want, expectation and hope.

He chafed his arms as if this would still his thrumming heart. He reflected apropos of everything that most men would find it strange to be excited about meeting another man. They would say it was wrong. Yet John Watson stopped caring about things like that the day he died.

Well, the day he came *back* from the dead, if you want to split hairs.

He'd died for eight seconds they said, hardly anything at all, yet few men know moments so rare. As it turns out, eight's about all a man needs to understand that some things will never be wrong, no matter how many people say so.

So John chaffed his arms and hummed with the thrum of his over-excited heart, and John wondered what Sherlock looked like now. The last time they'd seen each other…was it just three years?…he'd been lean, tall, sharp-eyed. They had made each other laugh.

John looked up. It was just yesterday they'd stood so small beneath this big clock, giggling about pigeons, unafraid because, though lost, they'd miraculously found each other.

John wondered if Sherlock would recognise him. He knew he'd changed so much, though twenty wasn't as old as all that. Just in case, John wore one of Sherlock's old gifts. It was tattered, but still beautiful. Sherlock had sent it to him for his ninth birthday and, pressed inside a book, it had gone with John across the world.

13

Patting his waistcoat John nodded, a quick, martial bob of the head. Sherlock would know him. He would.

*

Sherlock figured he'd apologise later.

Ha, ha, he didn't know the half of it.

For what he was doing right now—hiding—Sherlock Holmes would pay penance to John Watson most of the years of their long lives. He would happily apologise on the anniversary of their meeting. He would smilingly crave pardon when a trip took them through Waterloo station. He would nibble humble pie if and when because, for each and every year of their future years together, John would pretend remembered pique for what Sherlock was doing right now, and so Sherlock would apologise for this sneaky sin with back rubs or biscuits or quick-stolen kisses down dark London mews.

Knowing that future of pretend-vexation and faux-regret, Sherlock would still do what he was doing: Standing on a mezzanine overlooking the four-faced clock, watching John pace below.

Sherlock wished he'd been wrong about the unwritten things he'd read in John's letter. But there each one was: The slow stride of a man still ill. The aching shoulder he couldn't help but touch. Hair grown shaggy because he could no longer afford to have it cut, and was unable to do it himself.

I'll do it.

Sherlock went straight-backed, breathless. He knows what people call men who have thoughts like that. He knows what people think of men like him.

He doesn't care.

Since the first time he saw a thing he wasn't supposed to see then *said* something about it, the *theys* of this world have been calling Sherlock bad things.

Crazy. Abnormal. Wrong. Freak. Queer. Odd.

He learned long ago that he's none of those things, so he chooses to believe he's none of the awful things they say about men who look at other men—at one man, just one man with too-long hair and a war wound and still the touch of fever to his cheek—and think, *I will love you better.*

The last time Sherlock Holmes had touched John Watson one of them had been sixteen, the other a year older. Aware of each minute that made up their one single hour, jealous of each that would come after the one they shared, the boys-almost-men sat under a four-faced clock, the sides of their palms touching, John's foot tap-tapping and Sherlock had counted each time John's foot touched his. There'd been hundreds of things to say but somehow the only thing that mattered was them, together, no longer lost. Side by side.

Suddenly Sherlock was furious with the distance between them, he had to go.

Go.

Go.

Quick as blinks he ran toward the steps, stumble-tripped down them, pushed and then there he was, a dozen feet from pacing John, patient John, *turning* John.

Oh John Watson would have recognised Sherlock Holmes anywhere. He didn't need a photograph or a description. He didn't need introductions or a finger pointing. Yet there it was, a small beacon: A simple round-rosy of pearlescent pigeon feathers in Sherlock's button hole, those rare blues from the wing that a small boy had spent years collecting and sending to his friend.

Of course Sherlock would have recognised John anywhere. He saw the long-ago boy in the man standing there, the serious smiles—how did he *do* that?—were the very same, the straight spine. Yet there it was suspended from John's waistcoat pocket, a paper clock-face, finely drawn in Sherlock's careful seven-year-old hand. Sent, along with dozens of others, to a boy who sometimes thought about clocks and things.

"You're big," whispered John, looking up at a man grown so lean and tall.

"So's your hair," Sherlock said, only a little bit breathless.

One of them thought about crying, the other about hugging, and even though there were people everywhere, so many people standing with them beneath their time keeper, John and Sherlock went ahead and did something else for one full minute as measured by a four-faced clock.

John and Sherlock held each other's hand.

Run of ~~Bad~~ Luck

Holland Walk, London—1985

Only an idiot runs in the dark.

John Watson is an idiot.

You wouldn't know it to look at him. Mostly because you can't see him. Nor can anyone else, for John's jogging up the steep, narrow, *dark* path beside Holland Park. It is twenty minutes before midnight.

Fortunately it's only pitch black near the top of the sodding rise of the sodding path on which John sodding bloody well finds himself. When he crests the summit some time next year, he knows the high brick wall beside him will begin turning again to low garden fences, the path descending quickly to the Friday night busyness of Notting Hill.

In the meantime John mutters himself forward, cocks an ear backward, carefully steering clear of bicyclists and weekend drunks. It is this last one he most fears, ever since walking right into a drunk man, rat-arsed on Black Sheep 440s and vomiting against the high wall. Then vomiting against John.

John huff-puff-laughs. Christ, that'd been a hundred years ago, before he'd finished med school. Before the army. Before the Falklands.

John shrugs.

It was like a tic now. *Falklands. Shrug.* It was an unconscious reminder from his body's muscles, bones, and tendons: *We're doing well, John. Healed up nice. Just a twinge of weakness now and again, sort of like a trick knee. Nothing tragic, maybe the occasional splash of tea onto our shoes, that's all. Better than dead, all told. Shoulder'd probably be stronger if you did those exercises.*

John huff-puffs.

Yes, it probably would. Get stronger. If he did the exercises the nice army nurse had taught him in Río Gallegos. It'd help if he did *any*. Exercise that is. He seems to have given that up too, pretty much right after being sent home half-healed. From the Falklands.

Shrug.

Which is why he's right this minute and in the dark plodding uphill. Huffing. Puffing. Because he'd finally got tired of being tired. Feeling slow, weak, disconnected.

But god he hates jogging. It's like taking a shower with your clothes on, it's like—

The bicyclist sees John just in time but not *all* in time. Her elbow clips him hard enough to twist his feet round themselves, then spin him in balletic slow-motion. John trips. John goes down.

The bicyclist never even stops.

A minute later a stranger does.

On his knees, Sherlock Holmes puts his hand on the man's chest, then his ear right up to the man's mouth.

Sherlock's often up close with the dead and the dead don't breathe, but Sherlock's pretty sure he should hear *something* out of the unconscious man. He doesn't, then he still doesn't, and so Sherlock clamps his mouth over the man's mouth and huffs and puffs, in and out, in and out.

It's been said by the poetic that a man can live a lifetime in just a few moments, and John Watson will from here on vouch for the verity of this.

Because in the dozen seconds the good doctor is dazed and motionless, he has a so-long, so-sweet dream. In it he walks barefoot on cool sand, holds a man's long-fingered hand, laughs at the nuzzling rasp of five-o'clock shadow against his neck. He hmmms happily at the press of a warm, laughing mouth against his. Time goes treacle slow for that fine kiss, a kiss soft and not, emphatically given and got, familiar and long and lovely.

In and…

…John sighs a warm breath out, opens his eyes with a dreamy smile—then shouts and shoves at the stranger kneeling over him. The man whuffs and falls back, his head hitting the brick wall with a crack.

For long moments neither man moves, both groan, everything stinks of city dirt and adrenaline, then Sherlock Holmes makes a long arm and yanks the now-conscious man out of the path of another cyclist.

John grunts grateful then quick-smart is so so sorry for nearly knocking his Samaritan unconscious. He scrabbles to his hands and knees, reaches out, "Are you ok—" and collapses, rolling on to his back, aching hand clutched to his chest.

When he opens his eyes, the faint glint of two wide ones peer down at him.

*

"—to hospital."

"I appreciate what you did, Mr. Hol—"

19

"Sher—"

"—lock, but I already told you, I'm not going. People die in hospitals."

"You're a doctor."

"So I know what I'm talking about. Wait, how did you know I—ow."

John clutches his Samaritan's arm tighter with the hand that isn't scraped raw, bleeding, or sending shooting pain into his shoulder. John does this to take some weight off the leg whose knee is skinned, gory, and shooting pain into his hip.

"But *you* could have a concussion, Mr. Hol—Sherlock, so I'll just nip into one of these pubs, use the gents for its intended purpose, then take you to a clinic I know in Earl's—"

"Thank you Dr. Wat—"

"John."

"—ohn, I'd rather not."

"You're bleeding."

"So are you. You're also limping and have a rash."

John stops and in confusion stares at his bloody hand, his oozing knee, his scraped shin, and Sherlock.

"Rash?"

Sherlock peers at John as if he is a simple but interesting specimen. An amoeba maybe. In three months and two and a half minutes Sherlock will have a cock up John's arse and John will be saying—at volume—impolite things about the inappropriateness of that look.

That'll be then, this is now, and now they're on the pavement outside a club whose strobe light periodically washes that pavement in a bloody red and Sherlock is gesturing at John's mouth. John touches the skin around his lips and winces.

"From when you kissed me."

"Excuse me?"

"The rash. It's beard burn."

"What?"

"From before."

"Before."

"On the jogging path."

On the...*Oh.*

What with the falling down, the semi-unconsciousness, and the subsequent bleeding, John had not only forgotten the kissing dream, but just noticed his Samaritan's two-day beard.

John reflexively clamps a hand over his red mouth, mutters, "I really need to pee."

A minute later John has not peed. Instead he is standing beside Sherlock in a pub's open doorway and Sherlock is saying, "Not this one. The owner's a kleptomaniac."

"What?"

"The keys, don't you see all the keys?"

A raucous crowd spills onto the pavement at the next pub but Sherlock keeps them walking. "The blood," he explains, "The manager will presume you're a brawler. He won't let us in."

Sherlock glances into the interior of the next pub. It has a roaring fire and comfortable chairs. John sighs in longing but Sherlock says, "The bartender doesn't like gay men."

Reflexively John clutches Sherlock's arm tighter. "What? Why do—"

Sherlock points. "That one."

*

21

"—and that man not only cheats with his boss *and* his boss' husband, he—*oof.*"

John is standing on tip-toe at the far end of the Blue Pineapple's cluttered bar. He *was* trying to dab blood from his Samaritan's brow with a damp napkin but instead he is now clapping a hand firmly over the man's fool mouth again.

"You see, here's the thing," John hisses over the hub-bub of the noisy pub crowd. "When a big burly guy hears two annoying men saying very private things about him, the big burly man usually wants to beat those annoying men up. But here's a thing I can tell you from experience. Mr. Burly is always going to start with the smaller man, even if it's the bigger man who has claimed out loud that Mr. Burly—" Here John drops his voice to a whisper, "—wears silk knickers and suspenders underneath his thousand pound leather trousers."

"Bdhedoes."

"Right, you see, I don't care that he does. I don't care if he also sings *Joseph and the Amazing Technicolor Dreamcoat* in a nice falsetto while he prances around. The thing I *do* care about is that you still refuse to go into the loo to clean up because you say it's unsanitary and so you're standing here oozing in public, and it's bad enough that the oozing is *my* fault, but it's also bad enough that me cleaning you up in out here has already got us looks from half the pub, the half you didn't tell tales on—"

"Ddoo."

"—deduce, right, *whatever.* Anyway, the point I'm making is what's mostly the most bad is that the moment you mumbled that little addition about Mr. Burly preferring purple panties, I think he clenched his arse cheeks so hard he did his prostate a mischief."

John waits a moment but Sherlock does not attempt to say anything.

"Now I'm sure you'll acknowledge that it was really very gentlemanly of him to do nothing more than call us both poofters before he went into the loo, instead of the much more expected thrashing of *me* so as to teach *you* a lesson. Now, here's the thing we're going to do."

John gets off his tip-toes.

"We're going to finish these beers. Then if you still won't go to the clinic we're going to have another. Then you're going to tell me how you know I'm a doctor and how you know what Mr. Burly has on under all that leather, because I actually caught sight of a bra strap under his silver-studded jacket, and then we're going to shake hands and move on with our lives. What we are not going to do is keep gossiping—"

"Ddoong."

"—deducing things about strangers, all right?"

Sherlock says nothing.

"All right?"

Sherlock says more nothing.

John frowns and takes his hand off Sherlock's mouth. Sherlock nods.

"Well. Good. Now let me see your hands again."

Sherlock hands John one of his hands. Presently he feels the need to defend the consulting detective trade. "Deduction isn't gossip, it's a science."

John makes some sort of mouth noise and waves a hand for Sherlock's other hand. This is given and inspected.

"Just a bit red now. They'll be fine in a day or two."

"That was the Men's Room Mugger."

John forgets to let go of Sherlock's hand. He frowns at him and says, "What now?"

"The person who just went into the gents, right behind Mr. Burly."

John blinks quickly a half dozen times. "The Men's Room Mug—oh! That creepy, menacing, sinister guy with the twisted lip?"

"Those all mean the same thing. And yes."

"The Men's Room Mugger, he's the one who keeps robbing all those poor rich guys in the toilets."

"That's a dichotomy. I just figured out why no one's caught him."

"Does this always happen to you?"

"What?"

"All the *crime.*"

Sherlock is about to say this is the first criminal incident to have occurred near him in over two weeks but that's when the Men's Room Mugger comes out of the gents, stuffing something in his back pocket, and John hisses, "That guy? That one?"

With the subtly of someone unsubtle, Sherlock turns and stares. "Yes."

The mugger side-eyes them both, then slopes out the door and magickes himself into the dark. About then Mr. Burly waddles from the loo, trousers undone, purple silk knickers with pert white bows just barely covering his essentials. "Hey! Hey! That bloke took my wallet!"

John bounces on his tip-toes. "You were right! His knickers *are* purple!" John looks at the door, still bouncing. "Should we do something? We should do something!"

Sherlock closes his eyes and sighs in a put-upon manner. "What for? Whatever we do, the Scotland Yard lot will take the credit. The Men's Room Mugger today, the Brighton Burglar tomorrow, the Hackney Hangman week after next. To them I'm an unofficial person, I'm merely a—"

A gentle whoosh of air signals the absence of John Watson.

Sherlock sighs in long-suffering. He puts his pint down, breathes slowly through his nose and resists the impulse for as long as he is able. This turns out to be one beer belch, two blinks, or a triple-time thrum of the heart, depending on how you count. Then Sherlock bolts out the door.

Seconds later he looks left, sees John Watson catch up with the mugger about the time the mugger is turning on him.

A knife flashes.

Sherlock runs.

*

John bounces down hospital steps on his tip-toes, clutching Sherlock's arm and giggling, "Ouch! Ouch! Ouch!"

He presses his splinted wrist to his chest and squints at Sherlock with the eye that isn't covered by a patch. "—and when she dragged you into the fountain I thought you were done for!"

"Well fortunately you're very good shot with a pair of trainers."

"Yeah, but I'm sorry that when she passed out she nearly sliced off your ear."

Sherlock shrugs, insouciant, as if the giant bandage wrapping up the entire left side of his head is some kind of rakish fedora. He pats John's non-bandaged hand and catches him when John trips a bit.

They stop to beam at each other. The eastern sky is tinted orange-pink with dawn. Everything is fantastic.

They lean toward one another at exactly the same moment. Their foreheads clunk together with the soft thud of bone meeting bone.

John blinks a half dozen times. Sherlock lifts a bandaged hand to the three stitches in his eyebrow.

They each look in opposite directions and continue together on down the hospital steps.

"They've given you the credit," Sherlock says.

"I told them it had nothing to do with me."

"And yet…"

"Never mind. I'll write letters to the papers. I'll call a radio station. I'll make sure everybody knows that The Case of the Men's Room Mugger was solved by Sherlock Holmes, who, with his keen powers of deduction and an even keener eye, noticed that the mugger was not actually a man."

Sherlock shrugs again but even with the eye patch John sees the man's lop-sided grin.

"You too," Sherlock says.

They reach the bottom of the hospital steps.

"What?"

"You solved it too."

Sherlock pats John's hand. John lets Sherlock's arm go. They clear their throats at one another.

"I just helped a little."

John realises that for the last however many hours he hasn't felt slow, heavy, or disconnected. Sherlock realises he doesn't give a tinker's damn who gets credit for the case.

John lives south. Sherlock lives north.

"If you hadn't—"

"If you need—"

They both stop talking at the same time.

The sky is an artist's palette of pale blues and pinks now. John thinks that it makes Sherlock's skin glow softly. Sherlock thinks John's eye patch makes him look dashing, like a pirate.

They breathe slow and careful at each other. Each shifts closer. Just as they again lean toward one another John puts his finger on Sherlock's forehead, then says solemnly, "There's something you should know."

Sherlock pauses.

"I kind of like purple silk knickers."

Sherlock grins. John closes the distance between them. They kiss.

The sun is well up by the time they stop.

The Art of Gay Wooing, By Sherlock Holmes

The Lido Cafe, London—1908

With moderate effort Mycroft Holmes can determine the statistical likelihood Ambassador A will aid the creation of a stable government in Country C.

With placid scrutiny of a company ledger, Mr. Holmes can find the single anomalous figure among a thousand unerring others.

A genius with the rarest of skills, Mycroft sees things both small and great and machine-quick can deduce from those things a cascade of probability.

Which is why Mycroft invited his little brother to take tea with him in the park.

I will be in the Lido Cafe at 8:00 pm this evening and invite you to enjoy this time with me. — M

Mycroft Holmes knew precisely what would happen as a result of this small note to his sibling. In this order:

Upon receipt Sherlock would meticulously examine the paper and its envelope. At the conclusion of his five-senses forage for clues, Sherlock would read the note.

Sherlock would be intrigued, for Mycroft Holmes uses the word enjoy as often as the words shenanigan or hanky-panky.

Sherlock would suspect Mycroft of attempting to do something Sherlock has forbidden: Find him a flatmate. Flatmate being code for a special kind of…friend. The reason Sherlock had proscribed this aid was because, he said, Mycroft had frightful taste in flatmates. And Sherlock Holmes did not require a…friend.

Sherlock would then more carefully examine the note, finding subtle clues pointing not to flatmate tomfoolery, but instead to Mycroft needing aid in some ministry contretemps. A man keen on intrigue, Sherlock Holmes will always prefer the dramatic motive to the drab if the clues point in that direction.

Though he would find a whiff of intrigue, Sherlock would nevertheless think about declining the invitation in favour of some 'experiment' or other. Why quite possibly he was this instant sampling twenty-eight kinds of petit four, the better to trace a felonious Bromley baker to a riverside lair.

And yet, knowing all this, Mycroft also knew that Sherlock would come to the park.

Mr. Holmes smiled. He quickly dashed *156 Montague Street* on the outside of an envelope, using his finest ink. He then sipped a bit of over-sweet lavender tea, licked and sealed the envelope, and gave it to his clerk, who gave it to the doorman, who gave it to Bobby, the young page the ministry employed for delivery errands.

Mycroft then wrote an even shorter note to another man. He penned the address with care and precision. It would go to a young physician at a small surgery not far from the Diogenes.

Dr. John H. Watson
Charles II Street
London

Mycroft did not take a sip of the loathsome sweet tea before sealing the envelope.

*

Sherlock Holmes tilted his head left, right, then left again. He blinked quickly. Scratched his nose. Squatted down in front of the ten-year-old boy standing in his doorway.

Young Bobby blinked solemnly at Mr. Holmes, and thought he was acting like one of them squirrels in the park. Bobby liked squirrels. Some'd crawl right up your trouser leg if you had a bit of bread.

The younger Mr. Holmes quick-blinked at him again, pawed at his nose again, such that Bobby had a sudden powerful urge to dig in his pockets for a crust.

"Thirty minutes if you please," said Mr. Holmes so quickly Bobby had to furrow his brow to understand. Once he did, Mr. Holmes pressed a coin into his palm. Bobby tipped his hat and ran off to buy toffee peanuts from the sweets lady in Russell Square. He'd bet the squirrels'd love toffee peanuts.

As the young boy trotted off Sherlock Holmes stood, slammed his flat door, spun on his heels, dropped his brother's note and its envelope to the floor, and put his hands on his hips. He tilted his head again, left, right, left. He gazed down his nose at the letter. Then the lanky man dropped to toe tips and palms with the suddenness of a tall tree felled, and squinted at the words up close.

Sherlock knows there are bugs in Regent's Park. Creatures with a surfeit of legs and a tendency to buzz close. Sherlock knows Mycroft does not appreciate an excess of limbs and erratic flight patterns. Sherlock also knows that Mycroft knows that Sherlock wouldn't know a gardenia from a gudgeon, ergo there was no feasible reason for meeting in the park to actually *socialise.*

Unless a third party, a potential *friend,* was expected.

Sherlock sat back on his haunches. Side-eyed the letter.

Surely Mycroft would respect Sherlock's clearly-stated desire to be unmessed-around-with as regarded flatmates he did not want, and friends he did not need.

Sherlock presumed the truth of this without struggle, as Sherlock is the little brother of a man even more genius than he. This means that the young Mr. Holmes has long since grown used to presuming things about Mycroft that he would not in one thousand years presume about anyone else. This is because Mycroft, seven years Sherlock's senior, has carefully reared his little brother to be blind.

Which is to say, the elder Holmes will do a great deal to coddle and care for his unpredictable sibling, and he's known this since he first held the babe in arms. Therefore Mycroft has wisely spent all of his little brother's forty years creating in him a single impairment: Sherlock believes nearly everything his big brother tells him.

When Mycroft, weeks ago, promised he would not meddle, Sherlock magnanimously presumed the truth of this.

This explains why now, in his cramped little flat, Sherlock moved past his suspicions of being set-up, instead digging deeper, this time with nose and tongue.

Immediately things got interesting.

The scent and taste of the indigo ink was exceedingly delicate, marking it as the finest available. This was the ink used by Mycroft for correspondence with potentates and politicians from nations both distant and powerful.

Sherlock tilted the letter, looked at it nearly edge-on. As meticulous as his brother's handwriting was, there was still a faintness at the trailing edges of the S beginning Sherlock's name and the one ending it. Mycroft had been pressed for time when he wrote this.

Sherlock sniffed the envelope, recoiled at the faint odour of that awful lavender tea Mycroft drank to sweeten his breath before ministerial tête-à-têtes.

These small clues, combined with the oddly-late hour of the park meeting, confirmed for Sherlock that his brother wished to see him not for familial purposes but about ministerial mystery.

Rising briskly, Sherlock tossed the letter onto the side table. Regrettably he didn't have time today, not today, there was just no opportunity to stop *today.* He still had five more black teas to sample before he could begin writing his notes on taste, intensity, and bitterness vis-à-vis tannins. That said nothing of those same teas with *milk.*

No, Sherlock thought, blinking squirrel-quick, he simply could not meet his brother in the park, there was too much to do. There was just…so…much…too…too…much……

Sherlock looked around his dusty, silent flat. As if a candle had been snuffed out, his over-caffeinated nerves calmed, his busy-work lost its allure, and a familiar emptiness long ignored but never banished turned his belly with its ache. Sherlock often admired his brother's ability to find diversion in things as static as numbers, as predictable as graphs, and sometimes, just sometimes, he wished he were more like him.

Whether the visit was for politics or the simple passing of a few hours, Sherlock would go to the park.

He wondered if gardenias grew there.

At the door there came the careful knock of a small hand.

*

A clement spring breeze blew along the meandering park path. On that fresh wind came the music of tinkling glass from open cafe doors.

And Sherlock Holmes stopped dead in his tracks, wondering if it was too late to disappear into the Serpentine's moist depths.

Yes, yes it was, for ambassador Ranier Mayor had already seen him. Flitting from the moody shadows of a willow like a monocled bird, the ambassador hastened forward, a full champagne flute held aloft, trilling, "Hello younger Mr. Holmes! So good the seeing you again after that dreadful business with Colonel Caruthers!"

Pressing the chill glass into Sherlock's hand, the ambassador made *drink-drink* gestures and shout-whispered, "We hope still that you will take our medal! Come!"

They walked to and then through glistening French doors and immediately the ambassador hissed in agitation. "Oh! That insufferable singer traps Mr. Holmes still! This is why he sent me to find you young Mr. Holmes. Come, come then, I will tell you of my good news!" The ambassador made more *drink-drink* gestures then asked sotto voce, "Perhaps you recall my pear trees, when you were about my country estates investigating? Well sir, I have it! The Holy Grails of espalier at last, you will give congratulations to me!"

For the next four and a half minutes Sherlock Holmes pressed his back to a cafe wall, nodded at ambassadorial exclamations, glanced about for his brother, and mentally broke champagne down into its chemical compounds.

"—and the juice, Mr. Holmes, it is a nectar—"

Of course palmitic and palmitoleic acid accounted for champagne's creamy aroma, the latter of which Sherlock had once successfully extracted from a half pound of macadamia nuts.

"—both piquancy and what is the word? Formidable! And yet—"

Sherlock sipped his champagne. There was also the almost-gardenia sweetness of methyl dihydrojasmonate quite evident, a compound that was a cloying part of the eau de toilette his downstairs neighbour favoured.

"—fought her nearly to the death I tell you, for I would not be outbid young Mr. Holmes! And then—"

Sherlock's mind again wandered down the gardenia and gudgeon path. He glanced out at the night-dark park, thought perhaps he could do an experiment or two. There could be lethal organisms running riot and undetected in the Serpentine's calm waters.

"—and do you not love them too?"

It took Sherlock one half second to catch up, then reply, "I'm afraid I eat only blood-raw cow's livers currently, sir."

The Algerian ambassador pressed both hands to his chest. A well-known connoisseur of brandy, a collector of rare French fruit tree cultivars, a fine representative of his country, and a staunch believer in vegetarianism, he was forced to take a startled step back, speechless.

With a bow Sherlock took that moment to glide away, though within his fine, stout breast he was scampering like a madman.

To a madman.

"Sherlock."

"Mycroft."

Well, a big brother. Same thing.

"Employing your usual diversion I see."

The brothers wandered out of cafe confines, breathing deep as if freed. They meandered along the Serpentine's placid edge. A duck warbled moodily.

"What I told the ambassador wasn't precisely a lie. A recent experiment did include my consuming over-cooked beets in excess. They have a rather bloody mien."

Mycroft raised a brow.

"I thought it might sharpen my faculties. Alas, it—"

"Mr. Holmes!"

Neither brother responded.

"Yoo-hoo!"

Both brothers willed themselves invisible.

"Mr. Mycroft Holmes!"

With a sigh one brother turned.

The woman hurrying near wore a white top hat, a great many pearls and, as if it were a sport among the crowd, held a champagne flute aloft. "There you are Mr. Holmes. I must talk to you about that pesky treaty."

"I'm sorry Sherlock, I had thought we would have more time."

Leaning slightly toward his brother, Sherlock murmured. "I can return in four and a half minutes with the usual diversion."

Mycroft very nearly smiled. "Tempting, but impolitic. Perhaps we can share a bit of brandy later."

Moving serenely away, Mycroft joined the Belgian envoy.

And Sherlock was alone.

Which quickly turned him as moody as the warbling duck. He made a rude sound on general principle, thought about leaving. He could always finish his tea experiment. Perhaps start the one with wallpaper. Maybe he could—

"Ah!"

Bored witless by his own make-work, Sherlock grunted. In willow shadows a duck replied. Sherlock grunted again, thought about experimenting with the ducks and grunts and groans and was for a moment even more bored, but then, then…oh then something interesting happened.

Sherlock spied with his little eye a man in need of a *diversion.*

The man's desire was clear as a brand new test tube, as compelling as a dancing flame. For the man had not blinked for fourteen very long seconds, as if only in the pain of staring at his talkative companion was he able to keep himself from weeping or running pell-mell.

And then a flurry of blinks and it was clear to Sherlock the man was looking right at him. His expression beseeching, wry, and knowing all at once. It was a fascinating face, expressive, unguarded.

The man smiled and Sherlock smiled back, gaze flick-flicking up, down, all around, taking in the man's broad shoulders, smooth brow, his smile, close-lipped but ready. It was clear he had a soldier's posture, a surgeon's economy of gesture, and a great deal of self-containment. Sherlock was besotted instantly.

This last was *not* yet clear to Sherlock, though it didn't stop it from being true.

With a lift of his chin and a nod, Sherlock drifted over to the doctor-soldier in time to hear him reply to his companion.

"—so thin? Oh, well that's rather a long story Madam. You see I have had enteric fever—"

"Fever! Oh that reminds me Dr. Watson, that reminds me, did you ever see *The Fever of the Saint?*"

"I'm afraid I—"

"I played St. Bartholomew the Apostle and I will tell you we ran for three hundred-eighty seven performances."

"That's—"

"Capacity houses doctor, right on up to the gods, every night. Three curtain calls an evening and I'll tell you there's nothing quite like that. Talk about fever!"

"There was a woman in Luton who ran a constant temperature of one hundred and four degrees," said Sherlock, stepping from shadow and into their small pool of light.

Both Dame and doctor looked at him. One blinking rapidly, as if at a talking duck, the other grinning with such gratitude it had weight.

Sherlock grinned right back. "Mad as a March hare much of the time she was, poor woman."

The actor began to say, "I played the March hare in a production of 'Alice'—" but she never did get to finish, for Sherlock added pointedly, "Of course I'm not sure if that was her oral temperature or rectal, which of course would have been slightly higher."

The actor choked on her own saliva. Dr. Watson laughed. Sherlock beamed at one while the other fled. Then one man held out his hand. The other took it.

"Oh you wonderful creature Mr. Holmes, thank you. John Watson, and I'm afraid I didn't know how to…" John twiddled fingers at the long-gone Dame. "…do that."

Sherlock became aware that he was still beaming, still holding John Watson's warm hand, and that suddenly his own face felt as if it had attained the temperature of the lady in Luton.

A genius at deduction, a sterling chemist, a dab hand at singlestick, Sherlock Holmes was however dim as a duck about attraction. It took him a good three seconds to finally bow at the waist, shake the good doctor's hand a bit overmuch, and murmur, "Sherlock Holmes, my pleasure," then flee like the distant Dame.

The moody shadows of the willow proved irresistible. From its dark vantage a blushing consulting detective could do three things. Deny he'd just behaved like a middle school boy, give himself a sharp talking-to, and realise that the doctor had known his name. Had they already met? They couldn't have already met. Sherlock would remember the directness of that gaze. He'd recall those hands, soft and worn, the hands of a working doctor on one side, the sun-damaged hands of a soldier on the other. Perhaps Mycroft had pointed him out. Perhaps—

Sherlock would likely still be in the trees, perhaps-ing moodily to himself, but then something terrible happened. John Watson was accosted by The Honourable Mr. Justice Winters-Hammersmith III.

The petite judge with the big name was quite famous for two things: His meandering closings when at court, and his near-inability to perceive voices other than his own.

"—of course doctor, the phylloscopus collybita is a harbinger of spring, though you'll want to be sure it is this little leaf scamp in the gardens and not the willow chiffchaff with whom it's so often mistaken, a truly discerning eye will note a quite light-coloured supercilium. During breeding season the male performs a rather dashing butterfly dance for the female and I find great amusement in sometimes imitating it for my wife. This is not to say I don't have a great affection for—oh hello Mr. Holmes, I was just telling Dr. Watson about our little park denizens the—"

"—mallard ducks? I may have misheard but that is what it sounded like from across the way. If we are talking of mallards, you must have told him how the males have reproductive organs nearly as long as their bodies?"

The judge spit in his champagne. John Watson pressed a fist to his lip-biting grin. And Sherlock leaned toward them both. "It's rather shaped like a corkscrew. No one knows why."

The judge made unhappy noises, said something about his champagne. John Watson offered to fetch more. Sherlock Holmes grinned and watched him go.

The judge glowered at Sherlock as if wearing his tippet, silks, and ermine and about to pronounce sentence. He went so far as to open his mouth to do so, when Sherlock added pleasantly and as if just between the two of them, "Now the male smew and the fulvous whistling duck have quite astonishing anatomies. When you consider—"

The judge coughed into his champagne and murmured something to it, then said a bit too loudly, "Early day. Tomorrow, early. Very early." A swan warbled as if calling him a liar, and Sherlock waved politely as the judge's footfalls slap-slapped hastily into the distance.

Sherlock beamed at the swan, her white breast just visible in the spill of the cafe's warm light. "I'm afraid I have the sense of humour of a middle school boy," he informed her, then flushed in recollection.

As if on instinct he turned to look for the good doctor only to find him quite literally backed against the wall by possibly the most stunning creature Sherlock had ever seen.

He knew the face. Its sharp-boned beauty was on the cover of the sensational papers more days than it was not. Tall as a reed, lean in a way opera singers rarely are, the man had a face for the ages, a voice for heaven, a Brobdingnagian ego, and—it was *quite, quite* obvious—no sense of personal space whatsoever.

With a narrowing gaze and a lightness of foot, Sherlock Holmes went stealth.

"—you've an appealing tenor Dr. Watson, your speaking voice quite deep and pleasing. I've a good ear and would be willing to wager you'd have a nice little singing voice if caring for the hoi polloi ever grows dull."

A swan honked a warning. The singer did not hear.

"Perhaps you'd do well singing in a Greek chorus, dressed in a fetching little gladiator costume." The vain beauty tittered. "Now I myself have an impressive range, though it is in the key of F that I find my voice has its natural register."

Sherlock Holmes surfaced suddenly, like a duck popping up from placid waters. The singer took a startled step back.

"Pollen-collecting carder bees buzz a fine A note," Sherlock said brightly. "Though when provoked it's more between a B and C."

The singer blinked.

"And like yourself, houseflies buzz in the key of F. A housefly also carries the eggs of parasitic worms and prefers laying them in a putrefied corpse rather than a fresh one."

The singer wrinkled his nose at Sherlock as if *he* were a putrefied corpse, then looked at John expectantly.

John looked at the singer. Then he said, as if discussing particularly fine weather. "Houseflies are also vectors for cholera, typhoid, and dysentery."

The singer looked to Sherlock, as if in blame. Sherlock looked at John and beamed.

As if drawn to this miasma of discomfort and blooming desires, a countess, a prince, and a potentate wandered near, all in time to hear, "—ah but Dr. Watson, you forget that blood spray resulting from a massive blow to the head would—" and by the time all beat a hasty retreat they could only just register, "—though the brain matter doesn't usually travel as extensively."

It was not until John mentioned something intriguing about algor mortis and Sherlock answered with something regarding livor mortis that both registered the absence of everyone else.

Then it was not until John said something about tobacco and Sherlock replied with something about ash that doctor and detective became aware they were quite alone by the Serpentine, the cafe's doors were firmly shut, and those few spied through the glass seemed in a tight and distant cluster.

After a pregnant pause, John said, "You have the appropriate opinion on Trichinopoly cigars and an intriguingly wrong one on de Quincey. For my part I have a flask of good Irish whisky in my coat pocket if you're interested."

Sherlock glanced toward the pocket with the flask, though the doctor had not yet reached for it. Then he said, "You speak cheerful lies and solemn truths, listen close, but pleasantly ignore what you don't wish to hear. You are remarkably polite, but take to juvenile enthusiasms like bating the pompous. Of course I'm interested."

Because they understood that each of them was saying something else entirely, both men began walking from the small cafe and onto the park's dark paths.

"My apologies if you didn't actually require rescue. Mr. Bryce was…"

Sherlock did not say that the singer was stunning as a swan though perhaps of less brain, but he paused long enough for John to finish his sentence for him.

"…an exceedingly handsome man? Yes, well."

The pause that followed could not be called pregnant for no pause followed. Sherlock said immediately, "Ah."

Just as quickly John replied. "Was that you arriving at a deduction, Mr. Holmes? Your brother may have mentioned the tendency."

Sherlock Holmes was not a man for teasing apart the delicate web of polite conversation. His patience is applied best to things that rot, burn, bubble, or run willy-nilly down dark alleys. So as regards the art of tête-à-tête Sherlock takes the straightforward approach where possible. As they were alone, it was possible.

Which is to say Sherlock Holmes outted them both.

"Did your remark about Mr. Bryce's charms lead me to the deduction that you are an invert Dr. Watson? Not at all. I deduced that certainty with your remark about the flies."

Now Sherlock paused. It was rather a tic with him. So often after he makes a personal deduction, the person about whom he has made it tends to interrupt in strident terms. At the good doctor's continued silence, Sherlock continued.

"No, my deduction was that, as you seem to prefer a dashing sort of man, you would not, alas, prefer me." Here and by way of explanation, Holmes gestured at his own rangy body and somewhat extravagant nose.

For John Watson a bullet is a bullet, a fool is a fool, and an arse is anyone who defines love as something other than a mutual way to make two people joyful.

So John appreciated Sherlock's daring in not only acknowledging their mutual homosexuality, but in letting him know that should he find Sherlock interesting, Sherlock was interested.

"With such a fine brain and your roguish charm you need not be particularly pretty Mr. Holmes."

In the darkness John's shoulder brush, brush, brushed against Sherlock's, and the good doctor whispered, "So isn't it my good fortune that you are?"

To save his companion from any mendacious replies, John let their shoulders press together again and asked, "Were they true, all those things you said? About the flies and the ducks and such?"

Sherlock Holmes was busy processing rare data. The compliment to his looks was appreciated and informative, oh yes it was, but the touching, oh the touching. Sherlock is rarely touched and therefore rarely has such data to process. So he was quite busy parsing the feel of heat through John's summer suit, the sense of comfort from the press of that solid shoulder, when he realised John had asked questions. He hitched a step, frowned through several possible replies, then apparently offered all of them. "Yes. No. Some of it I made up."

John's shoulder did not lightly brush Sherlock's again, it pressed and seemed to stay. "Why?"

A fresh host of replies were examined, these for longer than the first batch. Eventually Sherlock settled on the riskiest though the most true, for Sherlock Holmes has always been nearly as brave as he is smart.

"I wanted to woo you."

In the darkness of the water reeds a swan chuckled. In the darkness John Watson clasped his hands behind his back, as if to withdraw. Then instead the good doctor did something unusual, a thing so difficult even Sherlock Holmes could not often do it.

John Watson proved he absolutely, truly, and completely did not care.

Wait. No. No, no, that's not right. John cared about plenty of things, including the fact that this fine-looking gentleman with the sharp eyes, delicate fingers, and a tendency to say fantastical things seemed to desire his attention. About these things John cared a great deal. The thing John did *not* care about is what the hell anyone else thought about it. He went on to make that clear with both word and gesture.

"Oh good, that's good, it isn't just me," said Dr. John Watson. Then, in the dark, the back of his hand brush, brush, brushed against Sherlock's.

After a few long moments John asked, "So which one was the lie?"

After a few long moments Sherlock replied. "The, uh, the one about mallard ducks. They don't have eight inch penises. Though Argentinean Lake ducks do."

Another few long moments passed in silence. Then John threw back his head and laughed, oh how he laughed.

And at him Sherlock Holmes positively beamed. "Do you...do you know anything about gardenia, Dr. Watson?"

"I adore gardenia, Mr. Holmes. I know of a spot in the park where they grow. Come, I'll show you."

Nearby a swan chuckled as beneath her in cool water came the tickle of a gudgeon, darting swift. And in a brightly-lighted cafe at the edge of the Serpentine, Mycroft Holmes smiled, sipping a bit of brandy serenely.

Sweet Talk

Smithfield Meat Market, London—1967

"I'll give you this if you'll give me that."

Sherlock Holmes blinked at the man holding a ten shilling note toward him. Sherlock had not slept in 49 hours and—he checked his watch only to remember he does not wear one—anyway, it was 52 hours since he'd slept, so it took him probably ten seconds before he could make his ears work.

When he did, Sherlock frowned. Because he was fucking *exhausted,* so exhausted he was swearing. Internally yes, but still. Anyway, he was dead on his feet and famished, because along with no sleep for at least 58 hours he'd also not eaten anything since—he squinted at the calendar on the bakery's wall, realised it was two years old and completely useless to him— well since some time yesterday if yesterday was Tuesday.

"Twenty. I'll give you twenty shillings." The man standing in front of Sherlock, held out another note. Without realising his mouth was open much less moving Sherlock looked hard at the new note and said, "Leatherworker, high end fetish gear, may have a shop in Leadenhall Market or frequents the area, likes espresso."

John H. Watson, at the end of whose arm those notes drooped, blinked at the man who had just rattled off what sounded like English but was in its totality so absurd that John was pretty sure it was a foreign language, or maybe he'd blacked out for a few seconds. No surprise there. He does that after a triple shift in outpatients. One reason he doesn't drive anything more dangerous than his own legs.

"I have no idea what you just said but I will give you thirty shilling for that almond croissant. I swear to god."

John Watson pulled out his billfold again, fished from it another ten shillings, shoved his billfold back in his pocket by way of dropping it on the floor. Didn't notice. He sniffed mightily because somehow it kept his eyes open. He waved his money.

The second note was still on top. Sherlock blinked at it and shouted, "Tea!" He jumped, then whispered. "Not espresso, tea. The leatherworker likes strong black tea."

Sand and sea, bread and butter, black and white. There are some things humans group together, the one with the other, natural pairs.

Though they did not realise, right here, right now, was the exact moment that these two men began tip-toeing away from who they were, to who they would from this day forward be.

John Watson and Sherlock Holmes.

Holmes and Watson.

John and Sherlock.

A natural pair.

That first small step was as simple as it was rare. John Watson looked at the ten shilling note in his hand, the one his friend had given him yesterday when he visited her high-end fetish shop tucked behind Leadenhall Market. Jessie'd needed change for the till. He'd had a pocketful. In exchange she'd given him this note on which she'd earlier sketched one of her designs—"Look at this one Johnny, it'll be sheepskin suede shot through with metalwork, the best thing I've done"—drawing with a fountain pen full of the bespoke grey ink she bought from the penturner a dozen doors up.

This by way of explaining that John knew the tall man had got it all right. He'd barely glanced at something and seen everything.

And John Watson didn't give a shit.

No, that's not right. He cared a great deal but…the rare, amazing, fantastic thing was that John witnessed a wonder, was in the presence of a miracle…and *moved on.* He saw and observed the improbable thing that had just happened and, instead of doing what most did, discounting, disbelieving, muttering *impossible,* John metaphorically shrugged *okay sure,* and continued with the business at hand.

"Great, yes, maybe I'll introduce you to her. She's nice. Likes tall blokes actually." John waved the thirty shillings at the tall bloke. "Just…I need that…croiss—oh…"

John's arm dropped to his side. The money drifted to the floor from suddenly-weak fingers. He stumbled back, all at once every last scrap of Watsonian iron gone from his spine.

Hands on knees, pretty sure he was going to vomit or pass out from low blood sugar, John panted and breathed and breathed and panted. Then his knees gave in at exactly the moment a chair was beneath him.

John opened his eyes. The bakery was bright. Sharp bright. Harsh bright. Headache bright. "Did I just pass out?"

He was talking to himself. No one was at the other side of the cafe table in front of him. It was five minutes past six on a frigid winter night and he was sitting in an uncomfortable bentwood chair sweating. His nose was also running and—

48

Suddenly a silver tray appeared in front of John. On that tray were his wallet and three beverages cold and hot and wonderful. John fell on them like a hungry bear and the analogy isn't far wrong because when the tall man set the tray down and hovered too close John growled. Horrified at his own behaviour, he apologised profusely while wrapping his arms defensively around the tray.

The tall man disappeared.

John had consumed the cucumber seltzer, the water, and was busy burning his tongue on the tea when the man returned with another tray.

There was food on this one and John looked at it and the remaining tea on his tray as if being forced to choose which child to save from alien abduction.

Before he had to decide, the tall man vanished again and in some part of his brain John wondered if he was repeatedly imagining the guy or passing out a little and just losing track of him. Didn't matter. He was burping seltzer by the time the man returned.

The man bore a final tray, this one with an empty espresso cup tipped on its side, and two drained glasses of water. He'd clearly consumed all three in the eight foot journey back to the table. He stood beside it.

John looked up at the man. The man looked down at John. The man noticed John's dirty fingernails, the army signet ring worn twisted wrong way round, and the scent of industrial cleaner. Without a glance at the hospital across the road he said, "Tell them a war wound is why you're no longer a surgeon. Maybe they'll be kinder, the other surg—"

John scowled. The man shut up. He stood tall. Then, like a machine automated, he placed his tray on the table, stepped back, turned. Left.

For three seconds John Watson stared at the space where the man had been and wondered if he'd hallucinated everything. The moon helpfully peeped up from behind St. Bart's, glinted on the silver tray freighted with sandwiches and the last almond croissant.

John turned toward the counter, gestured. "That man, he's the one, the guy from the papers?"

The baker shrugged. "Yeah, the one never tells how he does those impossible things he does." The baker made a rude noise, discounting, disbelieving.

John rose so fast he tipped over his miserable chair. "Cucumber seltzer," he said. "It's foul. Everyone hates it. I bought it for a friend once and she spit it out. I love it. He knew." John dug the now-crumpled ten shilling note from his pocket, waved it fiercely. "He knew." Gestured at St. Bart's. "Knew everything. Didn't you *listen?* "

John didn't listen for the baker's reply.

*

"Fuck."

Standing on the pavement, breathing as if he'd run a dozen miles not twice that many feet, John was furious at the stupid baker whom he'd stupidly tried to make less stupid. *Now* how the hell would he find the—

Smithfield Market. Just there to the left, someone tall disappearing into the shadows of its great arch.

John ran.

And quick-smart fetched up into cold grey dark.

It was a winter night in the middle of the week and the market was shut tight. No one working, no one passing through the long, arched opening, no one *finishing* passing through.

The man—Sherlock Holmes, John knew his name, they whisper-whispered about him at Bart's—couldn't have gone the entire length of the passage yet, even if he'd run.

John wanted to growl, vent his spleen wordless, as he always does, but he didn't. This time he hushed himself as if on instinct and that's the only reason he heard the low moan.

John Watson is a doctor. Was a soldier, once shot right through. So John knows better than most the sound of an animal wounded. Skin prickling cold with adrenaline, his muscles went slack for stealth. He would not startle this animal nor scare, no. He'd do what he does, whether in a mobile surgical hospital near Huế or in a hospital with a ridiculous clique of surgeons siding against the new guy, him: John would pick his battles, the ones worth fighting.

Six feet, four feet, then just two and…John stood in a small dark alcove. Sherlock Holmes was huddled against its wall, forehead on knees, arms wrapped around legs.

John slid down the wall opposite, the alcove so tiny their toe tips nearly touched. John scuffed his feet forward until they did.

Sherlock lifted his head.

"I'm sorry," John said, stopped there. Because people use the salve of sympathy where they need it. In a waiting room he might say I'm sorry and mean *I'm sorry for your loss*, but what the grieving hear may be *I'm sorry you're* relieved *for your loss.*

51

I'm sorry their suffering was so great that all you feel is the guilt of relief.

In the grey light washing up into the alcove, John saw Sherlock blink his eyes wide. John blinked right back.

People tend to look away from grief and pain. It's too big a responsibility to see. If you see you must soothe and that's a crap shoot. It's hard to guess what comfort to offer friends much less strangers. But John knows something else: Just about any comfort helps, anything at all.

"I just worked three shifts at Bart's because food poisoning took out five on-call doctors and I'll tell you honest and true, the only thing that got me through the last couple hours was the sure and certain knowledge that even if I had to crawl from Bart's to that crappy bakery just across, well I knew there'd be an almond croissant waiting. An almond croissant, do you understand? I love them. Beyond all reason. If one of them had a penis I think I'd marry it."

Sherlock Holmes blinked his eyes wider. He stopped breathing. Then Sherlock Holmes choked. Actually, it was more a bark.

No, it wasn't that either. It was the improbable, the impossible, it was laughter, giddy and sweet, it was comfort from a stranger whose toes were touching his. It was the most ridiculous comment in the world doing what nothing had done for the last two days: Hushed his brain quiet, calmed the thrum of his heart, let him breathe without dread.

Only in movies do confessions come easy. Sitting quiet in the dark of a shut-tight meat market wasn't precisely cinematic and Sherlock was no movie hero, so he didn't at that moment confess what was going on in his head.

Later, yes, John would learn that Sherlock had been awake for the last two days on a case that had him deducing crayon drawings, tasting dirt, then wading through a filthy tributary of the River Fleet. He'd been pushed relentlessly by the panic of a dozen Scotland Yard police officers, a begging father, a silent mother, and the sure and certain knowledge that if he did not do what he does, if he didn't pull genius out of his metaphorical hat and find two small children before midnight—when the river rose—those children would be dead.

No, Sherlock didn't talk about any of that right then, nor about how sometimes he can't turn it off, how afterward, when he's done his brilliant best and saved the day and everyone's tipped him a quick thanks and gone away…sometimes he can't absolutely can't no, nope, absolutely can not stop and so he walks London though exhausted, he deduces a man buying oranges, a woman staring at her shoes, the provenance of muddy puddles, he roams and mutters and plans how he'll get Lestrade to call him sooner next time and he tries and tries to turn genius off but he can't, not until he's so weak he can barely stand, not until he's slumped against a wall and hiding in shadows.

"I found them," Sherlock huffed soft, knowing he wouldn't be understood but that was fine because that wasn't anything new. "Before the river rose."

John nodded. Because he knew enough. Work at Bart's and you know about the infamous Holmes, the guy every other person seemed to have a story about, most ending with, "I don't know. He's just kind of strange."

So yes, John knew enough, just enough to take another tiny tip-toe toward his *me* becoming *we,* so John smiled. "Of course you did."

In slow and sure degrees Sherlock smiled back, and it was good for awhile, really good.

Then Sherlock's belly growled.

John's smile fell away.

John growled.

Then John hissed, "Oh *hell* no."

Because here's how it is with John H. Watson: He's not going to stand for avoidable suffering. There are enough big miseries in this world without accepting the small ones too, so no, nope, he has not, will not, does not put up with preventable pains.

Which is why John got on his knees in that dark little alcove and he dropped a wax paper bag on the ground between Sherlock's feet, and he said, "The sandwiches are in there mister and you're going to eat one."

So, right. Here's how it is with Sherlock Holmes: He's used to people getting all up in his face, he's used to teeth-clenched attitude, and thunderous frowns. What he's not used to is all of those things coming at him like this. *For* him. To *help* him.

His stomach rumbled again.

With another growl, much like a hungry, *self-righteous* bear, John Watson ripped at the wax paper bag. Sandwich boxes flew, crumpled napkins, a receipt. In the end John thrust half an egg mayonnaise sandwich toward Sherlock and shoved the other half in his own mouth, biting savagely as if to 1) show how it was done and 2) imply what a self-righteous bear might do to a person if provoked.

Though Sherlock both saw and observed, he didn't eat. Instead he did something strange: he leaned forward and opened his mouth.

John stopped rending his food. Blinked twice. Then, as if this was how it was *really* done, the good doctor held his half sandwich toward Sherlock, until he bit down, chewed, swallowed.

And so it went. For one entire sandwich, then the other. Until both men were fed.

John slipped from his knees, leaned back against the wall again after. The winter dark made time both heavy and slow.

John watched Sherlock's breath puff out white, asked it, "Why did you leave before?"

Sherlock watched the wind roll a crumpled napkin along. "Because you scowled."

"I…what?"

Sherlock got annoyed before John could. "When you see what they need you to see they *want* you to see. When you see what they want to hide, they don't like it. Yet sometimes the one is wrapped in the other and I forget to leave out what doesn't—what they—what—never mind. It doesn't matter."

John scowled. And right here and now was another one of those moments where they tip-toed toward John and Sherlock, Holmes and Watson, where me became we.

"I didn't care about *that.* You were right, they give me the scut work, the surgeons. The young ones. They think they're making a political protest. They think it was wrong for me to go over to help. In Vietna—" John shrugged a still-stiff shoulder. "—never mind, I don't care about that, and I didn't care about you with your—no, the problem with you was—"

John leaned across the small gap between them and made mouth motions with his hand. "—you talk-talk-*talked* and oh my god there were sandwiches and that god damn croissant on a silver platter so no, nope, shut up. I did not scowl at you, no. Stop it."

The grey light had seeped into their eyes, over their skin, so it was easy to watch each other smile, then grin, then laugh and laugh, and as soon as one stopped the other started him up again.

Eventually they went quiet, breathing easy. Then Sherlock said softly, "You're nice to the nurses," saying a whole lot more than just those few words. *I've seen you in Bart's. Observed. You're kind, John Watson.*

Sherlock dug into his coat pocket, took out an aluminium can of cucumber seltzer and placed it on the ground between their feet.

"I stole it. For you."

A confession, come easy.

As stated, there will be more words in their future. Late night murmurings of the difficult days that had led to this night, but right now John reached into his coat pocket, drew out a small wax paper bag, placed it on the ground between their feet.

"I didn't want it to get crushed by the sandwich boxes."

They both stared at the bag, then at each other. Each waited for the other to change everything.

For a long grey time it seemed neither knew how to bridge that small and final gap, then they both leaned forward.

John got there first.

He drew the almond croissant from the bag, tore a piece off, then held the delicate thing over the small space between them.

Sherlock smiled, rose to his knees, shuffled close enough to feel breath. Then he opened his mouth for that small bit of bread. When he closed it he did so around the warm tips of steady fingers.

Sholmes, Herlock Sholmes

Hotel Russell, London—1999

"I'm Herlock Sholmes."

The tall, drunk man smiled benignly at the serious, sober man in front of him. And then the tall man held up a staying finger, as if the serious man had interrupted him. "Wait. That's not right."

The serious man, Dr. John Watson, glanced around the hotel banquet room suspiciously.

John's intel showed him that Athelney Jones was over by the punch bowl, deep in conversation with a St. Bart's toxicologist. Off under one of the ridiculously bright lights Bengamen Hadid was showing off the ring his wife had bought him for his birthday. And Lestrade—John still didn't know the man's Christian name—was sidling up to the buffet and pretending this was not his fourth go at the Christmas biscuits.

Not one of the people John looked at was looking at him in a *ha-ha-we-sent-the-drunk-guy-over-as-a-joke* sort of way, so John looked back to the tall, drunk guy, who still held a long finger aloft and was now saying, "I'm…Shhhhhhh..."

John knew only one other person in this celebratory room of one hundred: Detective constable Grace Superior.

"……*it*. I don't remember."

John looked around for the DC and then yes, there she was, all six feet of her by the sparkly Christmas tree, meeting John's gaze.

"But! I do remember that I am a consulting something or other," intoned the man, swaying serenely.

Suddenly Grace grinned lopsidedly, made a small double-handed '*go get him'* gesture at John, then disappeared into the crowd.

"Are *you* a consulting something?" The tall man squinted owlishly at John, as if expecting an actual answer.

John had no actual answer to give and so he gave none. That was apparently fine by the drunk guy, who suddenly shouted, "I know, I'm Herlock Sholmes!" The outburst caused the man to sway again, this time with less serenity. He employed the wall to help the room stop spinning. "No, wait."

John was about to say something when the man pointed behind him and precisely at Grace. "DC Superior, the very tall black woman who you—"

John nodded, "I know who she is."

"That's good because I did not." Very casually Sherlock placed another palm on the wall, being as the first one hadn't quite done the job. Despite both of these he still listed sideways. "*Anyway,* she told me to come talk to you." Sherlock took a deep breath…held it…held it… "Deductions! I deduce things! And I deduced that you fancy me!"

Of the one hundred and three people currently present at this Scotland Yard Christmas party, forty-seven turned toward the shouting. After nothing happened for ten seconds except more owlish squinting on Sherlock's part and the fading of a blush on John's, most of them turned away.

That was precisely when John took Sherlock's wrist and tugged him from the hotel banquet room, down the hall, down another hall, and then randomly through the first unlocked door he found.

Once inside the small, dark conference room he started to try and say something but Herlo—Sherlock Holmes beat him to it.

"You can kiss me now."

John opened his mouth in a hint of a suggestion of a promise of kissing but he did not actually kiss. "Excuse me?"

Sherlock was rat-arsed right to his eyeballs—if he'd tried to do any of this flirting thing sober he'd have been dead from a panic attack or frustration—so right now he was happily hammered and metaphorically frolicking naked through a field, not one single inhibited bone in his body.

"You fancy me and I fancy you and people who fancy each other do the kissing thing and other things and so let's do those things."

Again John opened his mouth in a hint of a suggestion of blah blah blah. *"You? Fancy me?"*

"I almost never drink."

John didn't know what to do with this information.

"I don't know what to do with that information."

It was right then that the earth moved for Sherlock.

He frowned, pretty sure that that was only supposed to happen after kissing things and other things. Then he remembered he was drunk and therefore probably listing to the left again and so he took hold of the wall very casually with both hands.

"I have appeared at five of Scotland Yard's pub quizzes in the last two months pretending I needed to talk to Lestrade or Jones or your girlfriend that you were clearly mentally cheating on—"

John opened his mouth to say something but what Sherlock had said was a little bit true so he closed it again.

"—and I did these absurd things so that I could show you how smart I am. On Guy Fawkes night the only reason I showed up at the Yard's bonfire thing was so I could show you that I could make a bigger more burny bonfire."

John opened his mouth, though not to say anything, mostly just to breathe.

"But despite these peacock displays you appeared unmoved. Eventually your ex-girlfriend—who, by the way, is smarter than half the Yard put together but that's not saying a lot except it is—told me that I should just tell you that I fancy you."

John closed his mouth because all the breathing he was doing was making him light-headed.

"That turned out to be harder than I'd anticipated, which was why I came to this very boring party—although I figured out who's leaking all the best bits of ongoing cases to the press—and got extremely drunk. So. There. Now you can kiss me. Which means you put *that*—"

Sherlock touched John's mouth.

"—right here." Sherlock then opened his mouth and sort of dragged his finger down his own bottom lip.

The whole speech, the touch, the long finger kind of hanging off the end of Sherlock's open mouth, all combined to keep John mute. Fortunately his throat had no such confusion and proceeded to let loose with a small growl.

Suddenly important parts of Sherlock were very sober. The parts that allowed him to kind of throw himself at John, spin around in something of a ballet move, and drag them both down onto a conference table, where fingers clutched, mouths mashed, suited bodies started to grind.

"Dear god you're already hard," John whispered.

Sherlock panted. "Well you growled at me."

"I—I...um, wait wait wait." John suddenly stopped dry humping Sherlock. He climbed off the table. Took a step back.

It took Sherlock a good three seconds to realise any of this. When he did, he sat up and demurely placed a hand over the pretty tent in his trousers. He listed left, took hold of the table edge so as to stop listing left. "Why did you do that?"

"There's a very good reason I did that."

Another part of Sherlock Holmes was quickly becoming sober and that part was his mouth.

"Oh don't be tiresome, you can't betray your ex-lover. Besides, if this was a betrayal to her, then you did that six weeks ago when you had your long, emotional," here Sherlock Holmes tried employing air quotes but succeeded only in poking himself in the eye, "'talk' at Starbucks."

John opened his mouth to reply but a drunken, pontificating Sherlock did not notice. (To be fair, an abstemious, pontificating Sherlock also would not notice.) "I assure you that your ex-lover does not care that you are...that you're..." Sherlock's mouth was fairly sober but the part of his brain sparsely stocked with idiom was still pretty hammered. "...snogging me."

The good detective nodded curtly, then politely burped against the back of his hand.

John tentatively opened his mouth, then waited. All Sherlock did was list left a little more. John waited a little more.

"Are you through?"

Sherlock shudder-sighed, blinked slow, and thought

about that. Briefly he came to his conclusion.

"Yes."

"Good, that's good, because I'd really like to get back to the snogging, as you call it. First, I know that Grace doesn't care. Grace is the one who told you to talk to me, remember?"

Sherlock Holmes did not remember. He opened his mouth to say so but John got there first.

"Second, I would really like to get back to the, to the snogging, as you call it."

Sherlock Holmes opened his mouth again and again John jumped in, so to speak.

"Third and finally, I just need one important thing first."

Sherlock opened his mouth but John placed a single finger across it. Sherlock left his mouth open but nothing came out of it.

"For eight months Grace told me about your deductions, your mad derring-do. She told me how you just about dance around crime scenes, how *brilliant* you are. And yes, I watched you at the pub quiz nights and at the bonfire—you could have just said hello—and all that time watching you was helping me figure out something that probably I should have figured out a long time ago. Yet, despite the fact that yes, I broke up with Grace because I realised I fancy you, as evidenced by daydreams that have a dozen times left me breathlessly hard in a public place—"

For a moment it seemed that Sherlock was opening his mouth wider in preparation to say something but no, he was just opening his mouth wider so he could pant a little easier.

"—despite all of that, I realise that until nine minutes ago we had not stood within five feet of one another and, most importantly, have not been properly introduced. And no, you telling me that your name is Herlock does not quite count."

John took his finger away from Herlo—Sherlock's mouth. Automatically Sherlock reached for John's finger. He clutched that single digit in a sweaty fist ("It was not." "Yes it was. You were all nervous and turned on and *perspiring.*" "Shut up John."), shook it with the sober solemnity of a diplomat about to negotiate a disarmament treaty. "I'm Sherlock Holmes."

John Watson smiled.

"I'm John Watson, Sherlock Holmes, and I believe I'm about to crawl back on that table with you."

In lieu of a reply Sherlock Holmes lay back down and serenely opened his legs, his arms, and his mouth.

If at that instant anyone had asked John his name, he would not have been able to reply.

The Empty House

Talgarth Road, Barons Court — 1940

Fires were started…

That was how the radio reports began each morning, after the bombs of the night before.

It was an indirect way, a stiff-upper lip British way, of saying where in London things were burning.

Wherever that was John Watson soon followed. If the auxiliary fire service was still there that usually meant John was there with enough time to do what he could do. Sometimes that was help the wounded, because that's what doctors do. Other times it was clearing rubble from what still stood, because that's what soldiers do. Most times though it was John Watson—just John because he was very good at this—sitting beside a surviving child or father or wife, and talking.

He'd come close but not too very, and he'd say a lot of stuff meant to help, or something else if what he said didn't. Once in awhile he'd just sit and listen, though that was rare, because when wounds are still bleeding the wounded don't usually have much to say.

John understood that bit, about how devastation robbed you of your voice awhile. After the bullet he took in France took his surgeon's career, well John Watson was quiet for a long time, too.

Right, well. Those days were done but the Blitz wasn't, not yet. On night fifty-six of Axis planes in the skies overhead, their bellies giving birth to bombs and leaving devastation and fire behind…well after another day spent with the fires from the night before, John was dead tired. Fortunately, all he had left to do was get through this ruined and silent street of what was once a pretty west London neighbourhood, out of the drizzling rain, and thence not far to his bedsit.

It was starting though, he could hear it, miles behind him and somewhere east. The sound of engines were already thrumming in his bones, deep as his heartbeat, the drone of bombers.

More than the bombs those planes birthed, more than the whistle of their fall or the thunder of their detonation, John dreaded the counting. A meaningless one, two, three, a fruitless, reflexive four, five, six…he counted and counted each distant explosion. Even when the bombs stopped sometimes the counting didn't and he didn't know wh—

A bright flash of light, a boom, and for a breath-robbing moment John looked overhead and…this thunder was just thunder.

The rain came by the bucket then and John held his med kit close, protecting against his chest bandages and medicines and purpose. He ran over buckled pavement, splintered brick and wood, past the roofless wrecks of houses, then up the few front steps of the only shelter still standing: a pretty red brick thing with white stone flourishes and a wrought iron gate. Its parlour window glass was crazed with cracks, its door bore a *Danger! Keep Out!* sign—but this lone empty house was the only cover.

John opened the door and went in.

*

Fire is named by the things on which it feeds.

Surface fires flare over what's easy to find: windblown paper, leaf litter. Crown fires flash high up, from treetop to treetop. While ground fires? Oh those are secret things. They smoulder under the dirt and down deep, sometimes all through a long, cold winter, only emerging blaze-bright come the welcoming warmth of spring.

Sherlock Holmes was a ground fire.

He did not blaze yet though, young Mr. Holmes. His was a still-hidden combustion, short on fuel. Cases and clues were what his fire needed but he didn't know that, knew only that he was always looking for small and interesting ways to burn.

On this fifty-sixth night of what no one yet knew would be fifty-seven consecutive days of bombing, Sherlock was about to meet the catalyst that at last would bring his fire above ground.

Though not just yet. Not just now.

Right now was for dealing with an exceedingly annoying annoyance: the rain.

Flies don't much like rain, that was problem one. So the marker they had made, the one which Sherlock had been following in the dusk, it had thinned. Worse than that was problem two: the growing dark. Because Sherlock couldn't watch what he could not see.

Though the street was littered with the shells of ruined houses, Sherlock was nearly certain it was the stately red-brick house ahead over which they hovered. So, in a bid to outrace a sky turning from navy to indigo, he looked up and scrambled over, tripped on brick and wood and the ivy that still somehow managed to grow in a tangle between the wreckage.

A distant whistle, a *crump* sound in the east, then low thunder and Sherlock Holmes moved faster.

The dark and empty house loomed ahead and he could see, just barely but he *could* see, that yes the flies were there, over it. If he moved quickly there would still be enough light inside to find a torch.

"Yes!"

As if waiting for him, a regiment of torches were lined on the windowsill just inside the front door. He swept up two, tried both, slipped the smaller into his pocket then went still, listening.

He heard nothing but the rain overhead.

Maybe it wasn't the house, maybe it was the rubble back behind it over which the flies made their marker. But no, they wouldn't be so high or hover so fitfully. What they wanted was inside the closed-up house. It was—

A shuffling sound, and Sherlock turned in time to see a man turning.

Both stopped when they saw the other.

One blinked. Two tiny slivers of light visible in the dusk, repeatedly extinguished, then bright again.

The other stared. In a pale wash of torchlight he observed dirty army boots streaked with brick dust. Denim jeans covered with the same, a faded mufti shirt tucked into those. Unlike the rest, the man's hands and moustachioed face were clean, obvious even in the half-light. On his pinky glinted a silver ring with a familiar symbol.

The mufti and the boots, the denim and the ball chain tucked beneath his collar proclaimed what he used to be. The ring and the clean, clean hands told Sherlock what he was. "Hello doctor," said Sherlock Holmes, friendly as a neighbour.

John dropped chin to chest. He saw a great many people most days, did John, and though this stranger's body language was easy as a lover's, John knew he'd remember someone that…heavy. That was the only word for the density of the stranger, the gravity of him.

"Watson. But you can call me John."

Watson John then proceeded right on to a quick biography, because people panic less when they know more, though this man seemed far from anything like panic. "I just came from east of Islington. Were a few people in need there after last night. I was getting in out of the rain just now. Who're you?"

"Sherlock Holmes," said Sherlock Holmes, glancing east, toward a whistling, just as John did.

"Forty-one," whispered John, reflexively.

"Thirty-nine," corrected Sherlock, automatically.

They looked at each other again, fast-blinks wink-winking a Morse code that was, it turned out, a cipher for laughter. They both fell into a fit of it for a long, relieved while, then sobered when another bomb fell.

"They're getting closer."

Sherlock rattled his torch. "Then I'd better look faster."

Soldiers and doctors, they see more unkindness than most. So John Watson, who was both, could be forgiven for presuming the stranger's intentions were less than benign. Still, he was a politic man. "Look for what?"

Sherlock smiled and started poking around the parlour. "Flies."

Curious, John watched the man peer up and down behind curtains, wave his hands through the air as if conjuring, tilt his head as if to listen. It wasn't until he went toward an open bedroom door that John said, "You shouldn't."

For a moment Sherlock stopped doing what he shouldn't, flashed John another smile. "That doesn't mean I won't."

He disappeared inside.

At the near-far sound of more whistling and then ersatz thunder, John murmured, "Forty," and started thinking about not being in, in, *inside.* Maybe outside was safer, outside where he could see the sky and breathe. Except of course every day John saw that nothing was safer and no matter where you went the thunder followed, so it was easier right now to tip-toe quiet and follow a stranger into another stranger's bedroom.

"What are you doing?" John whispered, standing in the doorway.

What Sherlock was doing was tugging at a locked wardrobe door and maybe he'd been about to break it open, but with a grunt at the interruption he turned away, directed the torch over dusty woodwork, windblown papers, perfectly-made bedding, which he pulled back, only to expose more bedding.

He lingered his light briefly on books stacked beside the bed, their spine edges aligned one right over the other with military precision. Then he took a step back, flicked the beam down when he stumbled, shining the light on a shattered marble bust. He picked up a remnant slick with something dark, answered, "I'm looking."

He peered at the shard in the poor light, ran the slick stuff on it between his fingers, then sniffed. Finally he touched his tongue to the stuff and suddenly John was lurking there, right there, frowning close, hand out. Sherlock blinked at him and then, to his own surprise, dropped the bit of marble into the doctor's palm. "I find things," he added cryptically, then walked on.

John followed, the shard of marble thumping hollow on the dusty wood floor.

From the bedroom they went through the parlour again, then the kitchen, where Sherlock flicked the torch light over everything. As he did John trailed his fingers through the fine white dust that was somehow on all the surfaces in London now, and not for the first time the good doctor wondered not what the dust might be, but who.

By the time John shook his head from his dark reverie Sherlock was gone.

Suddenly John felt unmoored. Too light, unattached. As if, he mused, there'd been a shift in gravity.

That's when he noticed the rain had stopped and the moon emerged, making even the empty house warm in its pale light. The low hum of engines was no longer in his bones, maybe the raid was over. John could go now, if he hurried, he could be in bed before midnight. It was only a mile more, just one.

John looked at the doorway through which Sherlock Holmes had passed. A big man whose gaze was sharp even in the dark, who didn't seem the panicking type, who also counted falling bombs. A man who, like John, had things to do in this mess that the world had become.

Drifting finally to the kitchen door, John was sure he'd find the hall empty, but at the end of the narrow, dark corridor, Sherlock Holmes stood, waiting.

There was the soft sound of thunder-not-thunder only this time it might have been John's heart. He whispered two things.

"Forty-one. What things?"

Sherlock touched the door in front of him. There was the soft snick of metal brushing on metal and then the door unlatched, swung open a little, bounced back, resting on Sherlock's fingertips.

"Lost things."

A cold breeze sluiced past them and Sherlock lifted his head, sniffing the air like a cat. Though years later, when he wrote about the night they met, the analogy John would use to describe the moment would be...

...like a flickering flame at last finding oxygen.

With a glance at John, chin still darning the air, Sherlock smiled and pushed the door open.

The two of them stepped into a...cathedral.

It was a study, a huge room two dozen feet wide and half that deep, full of grand old mahogany furniture, floor-to-ceiling bookshelves, velvet curtains and marble busts, but it wasn't the extravagance of luxurious furnishings that drew the eye. It was the west wall over which a great arching fretwork of lead and glass rose, an immense, church-like window, its panes dirty with dust yet glowing pale with moonlight.

Both men stared at this impossibility. On a road where nearly everything had been reduced to nearly nothing, on a street where this house stood the only survivor, still, even with that much luck it just didn't seem possible that this delicacy had survived unbroken fifty-six nights of air raids.

Just as it was not possible for fire to live breathless underground for weeks, for months, waiting.

Yes, well thank god the world wasn't made only of things people thought possible.

Moment of wonder passed, Sherlock started shuffling his way through the shadows, sucking fast breaths over his tongue, rattling locked drawers on massive desks, tugging at the doors of shut-tight cabinetry. He stirred a regiment of pencils into disorder and grumbled a litany.

"What?"

Sherlock poked dust-dirty shelves and mouldy papers, looked up to the high vault of the glass. "The rain gets in somehow. I can't smell anything over this mess."

As if to make the point, Sherlock made a bigger mess, shoving musty newspapers to the floor.

Uncovering a long, hinged bench.

On his knees and prying a second later, he chanted, "Open, open, open," and when it didn't Sherlock shoved his face at the crack where bench top and bench body met, breathed deep, crawled forward, snuffled again, crawled—and ran into legs.

He looked up, "What are you doing?"

John Watson looked down. "What are *you* doing?"

Sherlock gestured toward the hall. "I told you."

"No, you said something dramatic and walked away. Then when I asked again, you said something more dramatic and walked away again."

Sherlock stood up, glowered. "Do you know why? Do you really want to know why?"

Sherlock might have been the one looming, but it was John's shadow in which he stood. "Yes I do," John answered softly, and then, before there could be any more mysteries he added, "If you tell me, maybe I can help."

When the next bomb fell the ground rose like it was breathing, a deep breath, long and hot. Reflexively they looked up to the cathedral of glass.

"Down?"

"This part of London's on an aquifer. None of these flats should have basements. Oh."

Just because you shouldn't, doesn't mean you won't.

Dig a hole near a river and ground water seeps in like blood to fill it. But you can outwit the water if you keep digging, though it's difficult work, expensive. Which maybe wouldn't matter to someone who filled their home with mahogany furniture and marble busts, to someone so afraid that they regimented their books and pencils, locked every wardrobe and cabinet and drawer.

The glass above them tinkled, fine bits of rubble raining down on it and Sherlock finally listened now to something he'd heard before: The hollow thud of a shard of marble hitting a wooden floor. Sherlock grabbed John's hand. "The bedroom."

A half minute later they'd broken the wardrobe's small lock and were pulling clothes out, quickly exposing a hidden door. And that was good, very good, because the thrum was in John's bones again and chanting apropos of nothing "forty-three, forty-three, forty-three," he tugged open the door.

They didn't go even a single step before the smell hit them.

Now know this, John Watson and Sherlock Holmes have both touched the dead, seen them, breathed the miasma of their decay. Yet neither was inured, no, not yet, maybe not ever, so both stopped breathing for as long as they could, which with thrumming hearts wasn't really long at all. Then apropos of everything Sherlock huff-panted-sighed, "The flies, they couldn't get in, but the odor of decomposition, it got out."

John was already moving. Taking the torch, tugging mufti up over his nose, he pushed past Sherlock, muttered "Stay here," and went down into the dark, footfalls clattering and then stopping quick.

The cot was tiny, the woman on it more so, dark, fetid skin literally slipping from her bones. She was far beyond a doctor's care.

"At least three weeks," said Sherlock, breathing down John's neck, then stepping around, closer to the little cot and the table beside it. He shone the smaller torch over two pairs of reading glasses placed just-so side-by-side, onto stacked books, their spines as orderly as those upstairs, then he ran the light over the body, the woman's fingers weaved together over a cluster of keys, as controlled in her death as she had obviously been in her life. Sherlock did not wonder it had taken her children so long to rouse the authorities that their mother was missing.

"Sometimes they call me," Sherlock said with a low, slow sigh, as if the words were being pulled from him unwilling. "Sometimes—"

Another bomb, further away than the first but even down here the ground rippled, a beast moving underfoot.

John has helped to dig the dead from under bits of rubbish and from beneath hundreds of pounds of broken concrete and each time thought he'd rather die where he could breathe, not below, not under.

He took Sherlock's hand.

*

They slid sloppily down the study wall, arses hitting the floor, arms shooting out graceless to the side.

The moon was high in cathedral glass and that was why John had stopped here, right here, instead of going outside. Here he could pretend there was protection, maybe a little peace, and he could look up and out and he could *breathe.*

One. Two. Three deep breaths, down deep into his lungs. Four. Five. Six…a much better count he decided. He should start doing that, yes he should, counting each damned extra day he got to live.

He grinned and then looked at Sherlock beside him, but the man's head hung, eyes closed, all animation gone. John did a brave thing then, maybe a stupid one, depending. Either or, it had the same result.

He took Sherlock's hand again. Then, laughing, John let it go.

"What a mess," he said, brushing dust and grit off a big palm. "We shouldn't touch the floor, dangerous. You never know what's in the mess." Tidying done John tugged himself hip-to-hip with Sherlock, placed their joined hands on his leg. "So, that's the mysterious thing you do. You find people."

Like John, Sherlock counts things. Sometimes it's the number of flies on a thing until he knows for sure the number isn't good. He counts how many hours it takes him to find what he knows those flies signify. He counts how many missing dead he's reunited with families or friends. And sometimes Sherlock counts how often he's thanked for what he does compared to how many times people turn away in grief or disgust. That last? Sometimes it seems there aren't numbers high enough.

At the admiration in John Watson's voice Sherlock stopped counting anything and everything just then, stopped being made of bone and sinew and sheer will. He slumped, until their shoulders touched and the sides of their heads thunked solid against each other.

"Ouch."

They laughed for a long time. It was John who sobered first, whispering, as if beside him was a survivor, a child or father or wife. "That's it, yes? The ones no one else can find?"

The moon was too far away for its blaze to be affected by wars or blackouts so it blazed pretty as you please through cathedral glass, and maybe it glowed especially bright on two joined hands, on a clean, clean thumb that stroked over skin slow, soothing, lazy.

"It's all I can do for the living," said Sherlock. "Find their dead. Some people...don't much like that."

John held Sherlock's hand tighter. He felt giddy-strong, like he was made of bone and sinew and sheer will. "Well you know what I say to that? Fuck 'em."

Fires were started that fifty-sixth night of the London Blitz.

Four began in Angel, Islington, though those fires were doused well before morning. Three tried to catch right at the heart of Trafalgar Square, but fortunately stone doesn't much burn well.

People do.

Which was why two fires caught easy that night, there on Talgarth Road, west London. One took light in John Watson, one in Sherlock Holmes. Any other time, any other place, and likely those new flames would've amounted to nothing much, small blazes soon extinguished for want of the right sort of fuel.

"Me? Well, I think it's incredible."

Sherlock's thumb began to run slow and soothing and lazy over the back of John's clean hand, warm skin pressed to warm, warm skin.

These two fires though? Fuel they would have in abundance. They would burn for a long, bright time.

Exit, Pursued By a Bear

The Bear Trap Strip Club, Old Brompton Road—1970

Perspective is damn well everything.

If you've eaten dog food on a dare, tongue-kissed a snake to clear a debt, locked yourself out of your flat naked during a snow storm, then (briefly) died after a bullet to the shoulder in a protracted war, well a shite job doesn't rate particularly high in the *fuck my life* stakes.

So the fact that John Watson was once a sterling surgeon and a first-rate soldier, but was now a bouncer at a gay club in west London...well the good doctor knew things could be worse.

Besides, the Bear Trap wasn't bad.

As strip clubs went—and soldiers see more than most—the Trap was clean, under good management, and didn't water down the drinks or entertainment.

They also let John take time away to fill in at whatever hospital had a doctor out, they comped a good meal each shift, they even had a small weight room out back.

Of course the club wasn't all glitter ponies and hirsute men, there were things John emphatically did not like about working here. The long hours and short breaks rankled, but the thing that drove John a little bit slightly kind of nuts was the damned *nickname*.

Yes, fine, when someone describes a bloke as a "bear," you imagine a big, hairy man, broad-shouldered, leather-clad. So sure, six-foot-seven Big Ben behind the bar fit the image;

Sven the star stripper had nineteen-inch biceps; and two-hundred-twenty pound Tiny Tim with the six-inch beard and black chaps was as bear as you got.

Still and all, it wasn't as if John didn't qualify, what with his bushy moustache, shaggy hair, and a still-decent body courtesy of his army days. He even had a leather waistcoat Stamford'd given him—laughing, but still—after his first month working at the Trap.

So the point John would make if he was actually trying to make this point, was that the next drunk who sidled up to him and tried pinching any part of his flesh while calling him a 'baby bear,' well the very next time that happened John Watson, recently of the Fifth Northumberland Fusiliers, was not to be held accountable.

Anyway, *anyway,* no one had pinched him tonight, no one had suggestively offered to put him in their pocket and take him away, and now John's shift was over, he was eating a plate of fish and chips at the bar, and if he hurried dinner he'd miss most of *Saturday Night Jaybird.*

The strip club-equivalent of an open mic night—where the winning amateur stripper got himself a decent bar tab—it was the Bear Trap's busiest, most raucous evening. When John worked he'd be on double-alert, because there was something about nervous men trying to take their kit off that set an audience of *randy* men into an over-excited tizzy.

The shouting wasn't the problem though, for John it was the embarrassment. Because it's embarrassing to watch an awkward lad awkwardly bump and grind while awkwardly stumbling over his own half-shucked trousers.

It was worse when they didn't give up. There was the short, cute guy with freckles who came back every Saturday and lost every Saturday and as a matter of fact he'd already been up and, impossibly, been worse. Some new guy'd followed, and now there was a lanky bloke on the stage and…he looked kind of familiar.

Didn't matter. John pushed his plate across the bar, glanced again at the novice on stage. Ah! He remembered now. He was that well-dressed pretty boy who'd been nosing around the club for a few days, groping under tables, getting himself 'lost' behind staff-only doors. John had had to have a word with him a couple times.

Hmm. Maybe the man'd just been trying to build the nerve to strip. He certainly moved well, sort of predatory and delicate both, and he was tall in that well-proportioned way that—

Didn't matter. He was a bouncer, working here was a job, and besides John wasn't sure he was…that he was a…

John grumped, smoothed the bushy moustache he'd started growing last summer, after watching the BBC's coverage of riots in a place called Stonewall. The moustache that for John had started as a kind of costume. A trying on. A question mark.

Well, am I?

Thing is, the face fuzz hadn't really provided the answer. Not after those New York riots had calmed down, not after he'd started work at gay strip club, not each night after he discussed his multiple identity crises with himself—are you a surgeon if you can no longer operate? are you straight because you've always said you are?

Never mind, didn't matter. John had an evening of bad telly and good medical journals in front of him and he could always figure himself out tomorrow.

John slid from the bar stool, shrugged on his coat.

Then all hell broke loose.

*

Perspective is everything, Sherlock Holmes can tell you that for fact.

Swaying his hips under bright stage strobe lights, Sherlock slowly shrugged off his jacket, tossed it over the heads of the hooting crowd.

Though quite fond of sweets, if Sherlock's not hungry for cream cakes or all-sorts or wine gums, he will not eat cream cakes, all-sorts, or wine gums.

He ran big hands down his chest, over nipples, then undid the buttons of his shirt one...by one...by one.

However, if consuming a dozen crickets, three worms, and a slug will get him the key that opens a safe inside which rests the single piece of paper needed to clear nine Newham nuns of a triple murder, then Sherlock will happily eat a dozen crickets, three worms, and *two* slugs.

Lowering his chin, Sherlock grinned wicked, shrugged his shirt to the gleaming boards.

Though exceedingly fond of adventure and puzzles and clues, if Sherlock does not have to leave his chair to know the butler did it, the wife took it or, worse, the butler and the wife did it and took it together, then Sherlock will not so much as rise from his bed or don his dressing gown.

With an impish smile and a look full of promise he undid belt, button, and zip, then Sherlock turned round and leisurely. bent. over. A bright blue strobe settled prettily on his arse. He stepped out of his trousers, socks, shoes.

However, if there is a half-million pounds of rare rubies missing from a Raja's wedding slippers, hidden somewhere in London, and everyone from Scotland Yard to the KGB have been unable to figure out what borough they're in much less on what street, well Sherlock will not only rise from his bed and don his smartest clothes, he'll willingly strip those clothes right off again if it means finding the hidden hoard.

Sherlock faced the audience, danced the fingers of both hands over his bare torso, then hooked them into his pants and tugged down…and down…and down.

The gems were here, he knew it. This particular Irregular had never passed Sherlock a bad tip, so the only question was why he hadn't thought to get on this stage three days earlier. The view was wider, he could see much higher.

Sherlock stood up, buck naked, just as strobe light crawled sinuous over the bottles at the back of the bar.

"There they are!"

Sherlock jumped off the stage, leapt over a forest of legs, jumped over the bar, and grabbed a bottle of gin.

Half the crowd stood, the other half got more than shouty, and the on-duty bouncer didn't know which way to look.

Clutching the ruby-laden gin bottle to his chest, Sherlock Holmes hoofed it to the exit, and ran bare-bottomed out the door.

John Watson was right on Sherlock's arse.

*

John hated getting arrested.

The shouting.

The accusations.

The strip search.

The waiting tedium after booking.

The naked cell mate.

"Please take my coat."

Staring through the bars as if toward a fateful distance, Sherlock Holmes tugged a small, threadbare blanket more tightly around him. "Thank you, I'm fine."

"Your arse is hanging out."

With a great deal of self-control Sherlock Holmes did not check if, indeed, his 'arse was hanging out.' It wasn't. He could only feel a draft up to the top of his thighs.

Sherlock sighed.

He hated getting arrested.

The shouting.

The accusations.

The inevitable physical struggle as arresting officers pried from his clutching hands *vital evidence.*

The unexpected cell mate.

In the past such cell mates had been easy to ignore into silence, but this one? *This* one felt complicit. Involved. Had a caretaker streak. He offered his coat every five minutes, glanced at Sherlock's exposed flesh every three, fingers fretting on his own thighs, as if counting every goosebump on Sherlock's body.

At this thought and in a fashion not at all helpful, Sherlock's body rose up in bigger, slightly aroused goosebumps.

When Sherlock had first deduced one of the bouncers was a doctor he'd been mildly surprised. Then, when he'd returned on the third night and watched someone in the audience hyperventilate himself into unconsciousness—a condition from which the doctor-bouncer had, under floodlights, carefully extracted him—Sherlock understood the benefits of employing a man who was both.

What Sherlock had not anticipated over the course of the three days, was his visceral attraction to the good-looking man with the sexy moustache.

"Yes, please."

John stopped doing the finger-fretting thing. He rose, stood in front of Sherlock, then slowly stripped off his coat and handed it to his cell mate. He smiled, sat down beside him and said, "So, why'd you steal the gin?"

Sherlock placed the coat neatly across his knees. He told him why he took the gin.

"Rubies? Really?"

"Really."

"You could have just explained, you know. About needing the bottle. Instead of the nakedness and the stealing."

This thought had not even occurred to Sherlock.

"So you're brother's going to get the bottle back?"

"Yes."

"Dump the gin I imagine."

"Probably."

"Wasn't any good anyway."

One second, two, on the third they glanced at each other and broke into peals of laughter.

Then they sat in silence awhile.

After awhile of that while, John reflected that he'd seen his cell mate naked, seen what that looked like moving off at speed. He'd tackled the man to the grass over by the park and laid on him. Been surprised when the man didn't struggle. Then surprised again when he himself didn't get off the man who wasn't struggling. And now they were sitting so close they could feel one another's body heat.

Yet they still didn't know one another's names.

"John Watson."

One hand letting go of his threadbare blanket, Sherlock took John's offered hand.

"Sherlock Holmes."

They shook. They sat in silence again.

John looked at Sherlock's goosebumped legs awhile. "Maybe you should…"

"Ah. Yes."

Sherlock handed John his own coat. He stood up and shrugged off the threadbare blanket. It fell to the floor.

About one hundred years later—in time as measured by rushing blood, thrumming hearts, and lingering gazes—John held out his coat.

Smiling, Sherlock turned his back.

John blinked slow. It was about the time he was draping his coat over Sherlock's shoulders that John realised he'd long since known the answer to his own question.

Well…am I?

Yes.

*

Police Constable Petra Singh hated arresting Sherlock Holmes.

The shouting.

The accusations.

The inevitable need to strip search the man to be sure he wasn't again hiding vital evidence.

The complaints of his fellow cell mates.

Their shouting. *Their* accusations.

Then that brother who always—

Wait.

PC Singh cocked her head. Narrowed her eyes. Checked her watch.

There should have been squawking by now. A whole lot of short-tempered squawking from whoever was sharing Holmes' cell.

Singh peered down the hall. Instead it was...quiet.

Singh wondered if maybe Holmes was asleep. She gave that thought a couple blinks, then snorted a giggle. While in lock-up Holmes did many, many things.

He perched on the bench like a keen-eyed hawk, mumbling facts and figures that, so help her, always sounded like either French or Pig Latin.

Sometimes he'd pace and declaim and this was more interesting because he spoke clearly, though to himself. "—and I must tell Mycroft that Mademoiselle Carere is in New York, Mr. Etherege is most certainly not dead, and the parrot has the combination."

She'd found him drawing imaginary maps on the walls, using cell mates as props to act out something or other, she once even found him standing on his head.

What Constable Singh had never found was Sherlock Holmes sleeping, no matter whether his brother came to release him four hours after his arrest or twenty-four.

So.

Singh peered harder down the hallway. The extended not-mumbling, the protracted un-declaiming, well it was getting suspicious. It hived up the hair on the back of her neck and Singh's learned to listen to that hair.

Last time it prickled up all itchy she'd gone and found that unfortunate man under Westminster Bridge. That had been a bad day for everyone. That other time when the hair had done its thing she'd won five quid at cards down the pub.

So.

Singh hitched up her duty belt, rolled her shoulders, started inching toward the cell where Holmes and that good-looking bloke were. The whole problem with the hair on the back of her neck, of course, was it didn't tell her if she was going to find a bad thing, like what was in the bins out back of the station that time, or whether it was going to be a good—

Singh stopped.

She'd heard…something. A suspicious something. A sort of groan—there it was again.

Creeping closer, grateful as always for her rubber-soled shoes, Singh asked the prickling hair at the back of her neck *what? What? What will I find?*

The hair did not say. Singh was going to have to look.

Another step.

Another sound.

Around the corner and…Singh looked.

Her eyebrows marched clear up her forehead.

The good-looking one was…he was…Singh tilted her head searching for the word.

Flexible! That was the thing the man with the moustache was. He was flexible. Bendy. Singh hadn't known a man could do that to another man in quite that way. Not without bruising.

In response Holmes did a thing that made the good-looking one…Watson! His name was Watson. Anyway, Holmes did a thing that made Watson do his thing faster. Singh's head tilted the other way.

She was going to have to do something about this.

She couldn't just…just…

Police constable Petra Margaret Anne Singh rolled her shoulders, hitched up her duty belt, and took out her patrol notepad. Then she stuck her tongue out the side of her mouth, and started to jot down detailed notes.

Dear John Letter

Waterloo Bridge, London—1919

No one meets destiny on purpose.

It's not as if a man thinks one morning: *Today I'll begin a journey toward legend. I'll meet an entertaining, confounding, and honourable man and from him I will learn to be good, then better, then best. This man will change me, right down to the very heart of me.*

No, no one decides such things. For some rare few, however, such days do come.

Today was that day for Sherlock Holmes.

"Your friend?"

Heston Stamford slid from the cafeteria chair, drank the rest of his cold tea with a gulp, and gestured toward out-patients. Sherlock rose and followed him.

"I told you about John Watson. He used to be a surgeon here before the war, then he went to patch up boys over in France. The poor sod got shot a week before Armistice. Now it's him getting patched up over there and while he waits to come home I tell him about what's going on at the hospital. Since that's actually kind of dull, last time I mentioned that case you had, the one with the redheads? Then I told him how your old landlord suddenly started stealing things from you."

"He still is. A newspaper, a pipe, a few pennies. Always small things."

"Well I told John that Mr. Shawn's a nice bloke but now he's gone a bit daft like that and in John's letter today he said a sudden urge to steal can be a sign of a certain sort of derangement."

Heston gestured vaguely west, was about to trot off for his second shift, when Sherlock said suddenly, "Do you think Dr. Watson would mind if I asked him a few questions?"

"He'd probably love it. He's got a funny old mind that one. And it's awfully boring lying about in a hospital bed." Stamford quickly wrote an address, then disappeared down a musty corridor.

Sherlock looked at the scrap of paper in his hand.

That was how it began.

*

Sherlock Holmes had not gone away to war. The great powers had found it far more useful to keep him on British soil, and there they had put his fine brain to work solving puzzles both esoteric and vital. He had served well but he had served at home.

When the war ended, the good Mr. Holmes returned to his pre-war work with the ease of someone who had lost neither limb nor loved one.

As such, he was unsure how to begin his letter to Dr. Watson and after dithering for a dozen hours of a dreary autumn day, he simply started by starting simply.

Dear Dr. Watson,
Our mutual friend Heston
Stamford told me of your unexpected
suggestion that my landlord Mr. Shawn's

petty larceny might be related to an impending dementia. Regrettably I think this may be true; thank you for opening both my own and his daughter's eyes.

My name is Sherlock Holmes and I'm a consulting detective here in London. While I have knowledge of a number of abstruse things, I'm sorely lacking in medical matters and I've exhausted the patience of most of the doctors at St. Bart's. If you had time, might I call on your expertise now and again?

Sherlock then presented the case of an unnamed royal lady, asked an unrelated question about bacteria, and closed with both a sincere wish for the doctor's health and a promise that he would repay any kindness extended "with fine brandy, the Criterion has a most excellent selection."

John's reply was swift. He provided an exhaustive primer on the bacteria that had so interested Sherlock, then went on to discuss the entirely different range of "pestilent buggers" that had led to the infection in his shoulder. Finally he concluded with…

Now Mr. Holmes, about your haughty Lady. While there's every chance she is what she seems, entirely too well-to-do for her own good, the sort of behaviour you outlined is also very common in people with severe myopia. In

short, Lady Thus and So may simply be
trying to see. P.S. Simpson's selection of
brandies would make a grown man weep.

Myopia, of course! It explained so much and he'd been
more blind to the obvious than his client. Lady O'Hara's case
was as good as closed.
Sherlock's reply was immediate.

Dear Dr. Watson,
You were right and you've nearly
made me regret I never studied medicine.
Apparently a certain talent for deduction
will take a man only so far.
I have a superb idea: You should
set up shop as my competitor when you
return. This should force me to keep up
my game!

About here is where Sherlock's pen paused, for he didn't
really have a medical question to ask the good doctor. It took
him long minutes to realise he could write *without* one.
"Sherlock Holmes it's a wonder you can cross the street
unaided," he muttered, then plowed on, describing the latest
case, though the Tankerville Club Scandal, as Lestrade had
insisted on calling it, hadn't been much of a scandal. Still, it
helped to flesh out his note to the doctor, who must have
answered the hour he received it.

Mr. Holmes,

I don't think I'm much competition for anyone at this stage, besides, I'm more the helping out sort. I'll chat with the papers for you after a successful case. It sounds like that Scotland Yard bloke, Lestrade, takes most of the credit for your good work!

Over the next months their letters grew more frequent and friendly. London was a popular topic, as was St. Bartholomew's, and life after the Armistice.

They traded their thoughts on the London visit of the American president, women's suffrage, and the state of the Thames. Sherlock had opinions on the City's sprawl, John on the sainthood surely due all of the sisters on his ward.

Eventually Sherlock had another question, which he posed offhandedly in the middle of a long letter about his tobacco ash research. After remarking that he preferred a good Finborough cigar, John asked:

Has your client's friend been to Siam? I know we live in a modern age of electrocardiographs and antibacterials but leprosy can still sometimes be a problem, especially for military men. Combatants come from and go to many countries, some where the condition is endemic. I'd check on the man's background.

Sherlock hooted. "Of course!"

Though there'd been no crime in the case of the blanched soldier, there had always been that one bit that niggled at Sherlock and sure enough, this tied up the matter bow-neat.

My dear John, what a conductor of light you are! You were spot on about the soldier's background and helped me put a final puzzle piece in place. A most satisfying conclusion!

Sherlock didn't share the unspoken particulars of that case, of how he was certain that his client Mr. Dodd held for his soldier-friend Godfrey Emsworth feelings far deeper than friendship.

The important thing was that the puzzle was complete, the gentlemen in question had been reunited, and Sherlock could tuck away notes he'd left lying at the edge of his desk for weeks, never quite willing to give up on any puzzle until he'd put down each and every piece.

Adding a bit of news and posing a question about a pending case, Sherlock posted the letter. It wasn't until a post-case pipe and a leisurely dinner that Sherlock realised he'd begun his missive with *my dear John.*

"Sherlock Holmes, you're dim as dirt sometimes."

Well, nothing for it. He could only hope he hadn't over-stepped, for he'd grown very fond of their correspondence.

Overstep it seemed he had, for John's usual speedy reply didn't come. And didn't come. And didn't come.

"No, I haven't heard from him either," said Stamford, after Sherlock finally got tired of haranguing the postman. "Starting to worry about that."

A week later a letter arrived.

> My dear Sherlock,
> I'm sorry for my silence, I nearly went mad not writing, but physical therapy this last week has left me too tired to do more than sleep! I'm delighted we can write again, your letters are the highlight of my days.

John went on to discuss the dreadful exercises for recovering invalids, and though he couldn't shed light on the question Sherlock had posed, he did illuminate something else entirely.

> …though I can't help about that matter of Mr. Acton I wonder about your poor Mrs. Harris? What she is exhibiting toward you seems to be something they call transference. It sometimes happens when a person survives something traumatic, such as your client did. In the aftermath they may transfer to you their feelings of gratitude and relief. I present to you the possibility that Mrs. Harris has fallen in love with you!

Wounded soldiers often
experience this too, falling in love with
their nurses…and their doctors. Please
don't think badly of these boys,
sometimes a desperate man will grasp at
straws to survive the unsurvivable.

Though censorship of his letters had ended with the war,
nevertheless John gave this particular missive to Sister Mary,
who was more than happy to post the letter for him on her way
home. To help these poor boys survive the unsurvivable, Mary
Morstan would have done much more.

Perhaps Sherlock could have used the ward sister's
wisdom when he got John's letter a few days later.

Reading it through once, Sherlock tucked it in his
pocket, took it to Hyde Park and there he stared at it. He had a
dearth of cases at the minute so there were no questions to ask
John, no answers to offer either.

That just left revelation.

Bundled tight from a freshening wind that promised rain
or snow, Sherlock tugged a pen and paper from his coat pocket.
He discussed the state of his moulds, an interesting old case for
the Sultan of Turkey…and then Sherlock paused.

He made his decision and wrote the words quickly.

…and finally, John, let me
reassure you about those boys who cared
for you. There is no man on earth less
inclined to think poorly of them than
Sherlock Holmes.

He posted the letter. And days later got an unexpected reply.

> …unexpectedly be sent home to London in a few days. We never thought to send each other a photo but you told me what you look like and I'm sure you can deduce who I am from my handwriting! So, Waterloo Bridge then? I'll hope to see you there Sherlock.
>> Your grateful patient,
>> John H. Watson

The envelope had been addressed to *Dr. Sherlock Holmes.*

*

"What could go wrong?"

John Watson has asked this question precisely never. Because a doctor, ex-soldier, and a recovering invalid bloody well *knows.*

But *seriously,* what else could go wrong?

The first thing that did was John being sent home days sooner than expected. This meant he never received a reply from Sherlock.

Wrong followed him to London when his promise of accommodation vanished once an old army buddy decided suddenly to move back to Wales. John ended up kipping far west of the city, spending twice what his drab room was worth.

Then this evening John had tried setting things right, starting out early yet still missing the bus that would take him to Waterloo Bridge. He fell asleep on the bus that came after, ended up waking up a mile past his destination, and now, as he stood in the middle of the sodding bridge, it was raining.

After a five minute drenching the snow started. Big fat flakes. Very pretty. Until John realised he couldn't feel the toes on his left foot. If he died from frostbite on a London bridge after surviving a war, John Watson decided he was going to kill himself.

Yet none of that mattered really. What worried him was that he'd misunderstood Sherlock, that what he thought of as a quiet but very real revelation had simply been polite kindness.

And then he'd all but said *I see you as those boys used to see me, Sherlock.* Except John didn't. It was deeper than that, letters and letters more than that. It felt like, well it felt like lov—

"Hello John."

Well then, the final thing that could go wrong? John Watson met Sherlock Holmes in the middle of Waterloo Bridge, east side, and the first words out of his damned mouth were a startled, *"Holy shit."*

The second words weren't, they were a mad fit of giggles and then apologies and then two men grinning at one another and one of them deducing everything, all of it, the bravery, the suffering, but the deduction that mattered now right now was the one that said *yes, yes, I understood, I got it right. He is. We are.*

That certainty would come to John twenty minutes later, as they sat too close together before a pub fire, holding cups of tea to their chests.

"You know what the nurses give you when you arrive at base hospital? The very first treatment you get? Tea. I remember that even though my infection had already set in and I was a mess, I remember feeling such relief holding that tea, knowing I was going to make it home. Just a dash of milk, and still dark at that, and do you know what I did when I took my first sip Sherlock?"

You cried.

John didn't say it because he saw it, saw in Sherlock's eyes that he knew. "Yes, that's what I did. That was the funny thing about all of it really, on the ambulance train and then at hospital, if you could sit up, smoke, move about a bit, god you were so happy. For a little while you were happy because you were alive."

Then came the rest of it.

John nodded and Sherlock wondered how John knew that he knew. Maybe Mycroft wasn't the only one who accepted how much a man who *looks* can see.

"The point I'm making is I managed to make it through a war and suddenly the thing that I was most afraid of was you. Meeting you. I thought you wouldn't come. I thought…maybe I was wrong."

Sherlock didn't have to say *you weren't.* Because John could look and John could see, too.

*

Sister Mary Morstan falls just a little bit in love with each of her boys. She helps them heal when she can, posts their letters, opens their packages when they're too hurt to do it themselves. And if she's lucky she gets to send each one home.

The day John Watson left for London Mary helped him pack. There was one bundle of letters he'd separated out from the rest. All of them had come from one man, the one she'd said, "has that pretty name." That precious stack went into John's rucksack, the one he would carry close.

As she'd sent John home, Sister Mary had hoped. For John Watson she'd hoped.

A few months after the doctor had gone, Mary received a short letter at the hospital.

…and I wanted to express my thanks for how kind you and the other sisters always were to us, even when we were a cantankerous bunch!

I'm living on Baker Street now with my friend Sherlock Holmes and life has been mad as a box of frogs! If I told you even half the things we've got up to since moving here you'd never believe me, but they've involved a boat chase on the Thames, a snake, and a priceless coronet.

You don't have to take my word for it, the Strand Magazine will be publishing an account of one of our adventures in the issue after next. I'll send you a copy.

I hope you are well, Miss Morstan.

I am.

Sincerely,

Dr. John H. Watson

Playing Doctor

Camden Clinic Hospital, Camden—1992

Most doctors hate working night shift.

You see, the human body is built to sleep at night. An animal of the moon and sun, it wishes to bed down with one and wake with the other, and no amount of caffeine, circadian 're-training,' or overtired weeping in the outpatients' airing cupboard is going to change that.

Though a person *will* try.

In case you are unaware, doctors, as a class, are triers.

It starts with the effort to get into medical school, where the abstract reasoning questions on the UKCAT make even a smart woman feel dumb as a potato. It continues into that first year when in a lecture theatre of two hundred other students, an over-stressed man can't remember his own name, much less the causes of craniosynostosis.

It's no easier for freshly-minted physicians, who are ever on the back foot as they rotate from respiratory medicine to critical care to colorectal surgery. Then there's the blame that inevitably accrues to the new, the mistakes, the arguments.

And finally there's the night shifts.

Half way into his first one-week night shift, Dr. John Watson became certain of several things: He had made a dreadful career choice. The senior house officer was Satan. And he, John Watson, was maybe a little tiny bit prone to hallucinations when exhausted. Fortunately John's delusions usually only manifest as phantom laughter he could just barely hear, but he does remember once removing the lid from a tea kettle only to find its interior was on fire. A brave re-check of the kettle seconds later showed only lime scale and a quarter inch of water.

Bodies denied rest when they expect it will quickly creep toward such deliriums, as well as a lack of interest in food, sex, job. Even a ten-step walk to the loo begins to feel like a chore.

So, rather than waiting for an embarrassing incident, John, like thousands before him, found ways to cope with night shifts.

John did not, like the surgeon he met in his foundation year, employ tea enemas. Though Dr. Richardson did swear lapsang souchong 'cleansing' not only helped keep her vigilant through evening shifts, but contributed to a fantastic sense of energy and lightness.

While agreeing that she seemed refreshed, John Watson discovered that maintaining alertness by rinsing his rectum with a dark Chinese brew, then walking around smelling alluringly smoky was, for him, a firm line in the sand.

John also did not believe in 'stimulating his senses' to keep alert. Though Dr. Marcon vowed that pebbles in his shoes, peppermint oil snorted into his sinuses, and itchy wool pants made it virtually impossible for him to feel sleepy.

While John vocally admired Marcon's clarity when they shared a shift, he secretly found the idea of the man's 'cures' as harrowing as the problem they were meant to solve.

Then there were the schools of thought that advised going hungry; the proponents of mainlining coffee; the devotees of hiding in cupboards and weeping; and then there were those that invented new ways of remaining sane.

John H. Watson was one of these.

To be sure John tried many things that first year, of which too much tea was the only keeper. Eight cups kept him so alert he practically had to beat himself into unconsciousness by the end of each shift.

Fortunately it was the middle of his second year John happened upon a better way of dealing with fatigue and figments, hyper-caffeination and hunger.

He started hallucinating on purpose.

Which is to say, John Watson started to write.

In a fantastically quiet world, where people talked in whispers and moved like shadows, John invented himself fantastical stories. At first these tales contained a great many zombies. A hospital at three a.m. gives rise to such fancies. Not only does it contain brains enough for the feasting, but most of the brainy individuals are immobilised either by wires or weariness and would hardly be a challenge for any but the most inept undead.

Which explains why John soon gave up on the zombie apocalypse and started imagining adventures. These included red carpet dash and drama, secret spy stuff, winning marksman competitions, wooing his latest movie star crush, or making plans to visit Australia, New Zealand, South East Asia.

Eventually John wrote a bit about what he knew: Medical school and the army, but after a time he simply stopped writing these fatigue-staving fancies having little fuel to feed them.

Maybe that was why tonight—three years from his first night shift—was not a good night for John. Instead of finding a certain serenity in fantasy, a bit of peace in silence, he felt fitful, dissatisfied. And hungry. He was fucking hungry. Unless he had milky tea with which to sublimate he hated being hungry. It made him mean. It made him swear.

"You fucking stop right there mister."

John Watson has got great peripheral vision. His reveries about that winning marksman thing? Not idle. He's always been a superb shot and for that he credits uncanny vision. Vision that allows his gaze to exclude the extraneous and lock on, and you know what? That white-coated skinny guy at the edge of his vision is no skinny guy he knows, and at three in the morning in a dead-quiet hospital ward, you better believe you quickly come to know who belongs there.

John turned to face the skinny guy directly and, after he told him to stop, was gratified when mister stopped.

John walked to the tall stranger, smiled pleasantly, and said, "Who're you?"

The stranger slow-blinked, and that really was a bad thing to do because he looked *exactly* like Dr. Holborn for a second, which was really quite saying something as his old senior house officer had been barely five foot and round as a tennis ball. More grievous still, the stranger did not answer.

"You can tell *me* who you are, or you can tell Mr. Vard in security. He's about a foot taller than you and three stone heavier."

Sherlock Holmes, for that was the stranger's name, stood taller—not quite a foot though—and said with gravity, "I'm Dr. Gloucester, I'm on my way to cardiology, and I don't have time for tired little dictators with nothing to do. If you'll—"

"Name the arteries of the heart."

Sherlock Holmes 'Gloucester' made an impolite mouth noise and stood taller still. "Posterior descending artery, left marginal artery, circumflex artery, right coronary ar—"

"Tell me about conjunctiva."

Sherlock began strolling casually toward the nearest exit, checking the watch he was not wearing, as if late for a four a.m. consult. "Conjunctiva covers the visible part of the sclera, the conjuctiva begins at the edge of the cornea and—"

"When a man presents with a yellow highlighting pen up his rectum what should you do?"

Sherlock Holmes stopped, the stairwell door just two feet in front of him. So close and yet so far. He turned back, frowned at the physician that had walked so stealthy he was now *right behind* him. Sherlock closed his mouth, opened his mouth, closed it, opened it once more for luck and then finally just left it there.

John grinned at the austere face facing him and said, "Tell him to wash it before giving it back this time, because for god's sake you're studying for your anatomy final."

John Watson intoned the punchline for this ridiculous med school joke as if relaying the symptoms of septicemia.

Sherlock Holmes completely had nothing to say.

"You're not really—" John leaned forward, peered at Sherlock's name badge. "—Angela Gloucester, are you?"

Sherlock still completely had nothing to say. John would soon learn how rare this was.

"I'll give you ten seconds and ten words to tell me why you're playing doctor in this hospital. If at the end I like what I heard I may actually tell the police you were polite. Have no doubt, however, that I'm calling the police."

John Watson dramatically lifted his left arm, on which there was not any watch whatsoever, and opened his mouth to count.

"Patient. Here. Royalty. Tengku. Hiding. Illiterate. Danger. Must find her."

John Watson blinked. Closed his mouth. Realised he'd completely forgot to count.

"What now?"

Sherlock stripped off his white coat and handed it to the man in front of him. John would deny that he took it as if carrying around Sherlock Holmes' things was something he did every day.

"If I don't find her she's dead. The morgue is a few levels down, yes?" Sherlock blinked brightly, as if he'd just asked what was on special offer in the cafeteria.

Suddenly the impersonator was striding off. John watched him go for three seconds, then said, "Stop. Right there."

Months later John breathed giddy into Sherlock's open mouth, "And you *stopped.*" Sherlock would reply, equally breathy, "Right......*there!*"

However that was for a well-spent sunny Sunday many months hence. At three oh five a.m. on this particular Thursday morning, John was barking. "One hundred words this time. Explain again."

His back to the dictatorial doctor, Sherlock contemplated bolting for the stairs. He knew he could elude capture long enough to find the Malaysian princess before her enemy found her, yet knowing this Sherlock still did as he was told.

He turned.

"My name is Sherlock Holmes I'm a consulting detective who tonight received a communiqué from the Malaysian queen requesting that I ensure the safety of her daughter while she is treated at this hospital for an unexpected rash. The princess is six, as yet untutored in English, her chaperones have absconded, and Michael Brompton is on his way to dispose of the child at the behest of—"

Sherlock Holmes was speaking to a brisk breeze blowing in from the open stairwell door.

Seconds later he was clattering down a flight of stairs calling with pedantic pique, "That wasn't even one hundred words!"

A left turn down another set of stairs, a right down a long hall, the haphazard fetching of two torches before rattling down more flights of stairs and thence into a basement, through a door and another door, behind three stacked boxes, then on hands and knees through a dirt tunnel, John Watson and Sherlock Holmes emerged into—

"Catacombs."

John shoved a torch into Sherlock's hand, shook the hand—"John Watson, nice to meet you"—and took off through the pitch black, calling back, "They were used to house ponies back when Camden Market was full of stables. No one knows how or why but a hundred years ago someone connected the catacombs to the hospital basement. They snake under the market and along the canal, which is why—"

Splash.

Two men stopped, two torches shone down into the green water in which Sherlock was currently ankle deep.

"Right, that's why people don't come down here anymore. Left."

Left they went, then right, the darkness paled with distant light, and then they were up a concrete flight of stairs, slinking through the wide bars of a grate, shouldering open a heavy door. "Cardiology," John said, with an arm flourish. "We'd still be tip-toeing through maternity if we'd gone the normal way."

For the fleetest of moments the detective beamed at the doctor. Then Sherlock leaned close, pressed his lips to John's ear, and softly said, "Ten words."

Here are a few facts: Michael Brompton would have bested John Watson in any marksman competition. Likewise, 'Bullet' Brompton would have continued to elude Sherlock Holmes.

The very nasty man would have gone on being elusive and lethal for quite awhile yet except…except tonight Dr. John Watson met Mr. Sherlock Holmes and before they knew it, without fanfare, and for the rest of their lives each man's *me* became a legendary *we*.

And against that, Brompton had not one *hot damn* of a chance.

Here are another few facts: As if they had done this a hundred times previous, John understood Sherlock's whispered words.

With a soldier's no-nonsense stride good doctor Watson called to the stranger, "You. You've got ten words to tell me why you're playing doctor in my hospital."

From that very evening until the day of his trial—which would not go well for him—Michael Brompton spent many hours trying out different ten-word combinations, attempting to find the one he should have used instead of the one he did.

"Who the fuck're you and where the fuck's the kid?"

*

The human body is built to sleep at night. An animal of the moon and sun, it wishes to bed down with one and wake with the other.

Yet with the right stimulus the human body can adapt to an amazing number of things, including week-long night shifts.

If that body belongs to an ex-army surgeon on break and finds itself soundly stimulated by a consulting detective in quiet catacombs, it can adapt itself quite well indeed.

A Crying Shame

Anywhere Loneliness Lives—1952

There is no shame in tears. John Watson knew this when he was seven years old.

Maybe he knew it earlier, but John remembers knowing it then, that day he sat down next to his best friend, put his hand on the boy's back, and patted gently and in silence while Andy cried.

The tragedy was two bloody knees, Andy was six, and both boys were sitting near the river (they weren't supposed to be there), and they were alone (they should have been home already), and each of them had been told so many times that big boys don't cry (lies lies lies).

But because little John Watson was very smart, he understood there was never shame in crying when you were hurt, so he patted Andy's back and he stayed still and he let his best friend sob out the pain.

*

John was nineteen when he found his flatmate cutting at her arms.

"It's not what it looks like," Aruhe said, sitting on the edge of the tub, eyes wide and startled because she hadn't heard John until he was there, standing in the loo's doorway.

Aruhe was correct. It looked as if she were cutting her arm but technically what she was doing was scratching it, dragging the tip of a large sewing needle up both forearms until there was a regiment of long, red welts. Only one of the scratches was deep enough to bleed, but John knew all of them would rise up in tender-forming scabs later.

John sat on the edge of the tub beside his flatmate and asked softly, "Let me clean them when you're done, okay?"

Aruhe had cried then, and John had bathed her arms, and neither of them talked about it. Then weeks later she said over porridge and just the once, "I know it's not good. But it's so I don't want to do anything worse."

John nodded. He understood the concept of a relief valve, something tiny that let off a pressure so big that it could destroy. So John nodded and nodded until she saw him, and they finished their breakfast.

*

John was twenty-four and he'd just literally walked into a hospital wall at three a.m. on his sixth day of a week-long night shift. Like every young doctor he hated night shifts, until eventually he didn't, but eventually was not now, now was for being so hysterically tired he couldn't move out of the way of a motionless wall.

The break room upstairs had ice in the small fridge, so tenderly touching his already-swelling eye John headed there in a daze, except in that tiny room a young doctor sat on the even tinier sofa, rocking back and forth and singing.

Marty was crying too but that seemed incidental to the song, the lyrics of which were the entirety of page one hundred sixty-six of the *Cambridge Handbook of Clinical Examination*.

113

When Marty sang he didn't stammer, so Marty sang that page from top to bottom and hoped he'd remember all of it next time, and maybe another old man wouldn't die, because this time Marty would remember some very important things.

John handed Marty the tissues he'd been using to blot his own eye. Then, for as long as he could spare, John sat next to Marty and together they sang page one hundred and sixty-six of the *Cambridge Handbook of Clinical Examination.*

John forgot about needing ice.

*

John was thirty-seven years old and living in a council flat, and the weight of everything he had lost after a single North Korean bullet, of everything he would no longer be…it filled his body like sand, it made him dense, stiff, day after day it kept him still and so, so quiet.

Because John would not cry his grief at a vanished surgeon's career, a lost military career.

He would not mourn the fragility of his body, still too thin from the infections that had come after the bullet.

And most of all John would not, would not, he would not feel his loneliness.

He would swallow and breathe shallow, he would not cut at his body or do more than look for long minutes at his service revolver.

No, instead John would tell himself that grown men don't cry. To breathe past the pain. He'd clench his fists on his thighs until his nails dug into skin and in the dark each night he would resolutely not rock or weep or breathe deep or cut or sing or ask for help, help, any help.

Day.

After night.

After endless day John Watson did this. And did this.

Then one too-long evening he walked out of his small, ugly room in a big, ugly building, and John took a long walk.

It changed everything.

*

Arms swinging, long legs pumping, Sherlock Holmes ran hard, fast, and focused. He would get her, oh my yes.

Ah, good! The thief had turned left, running right toward a night-quiet building site. She probably thought the dark would hide her. What the dark would do, Sherlock knew, was *confuse* her. The panicking pursued are so often more clumsy in shadow than the pursuer.

Sherlock ran faster, laughing at his own puffery, because my oh my he did so love the overblown, the grand, the sensational. Out of his mouth might come reason, logic, scientific precision, but in his heart Sherlock was often a boy at play, sometimes a hero. He was an actor, a magician, ringing down the curtain or curling the cape, unveiling solutions to confounding puzzles, doing what no one else could do.

His own laughter spurred him on and then, like a benediction, good got suddenly better because the thief veered deeper into the building site and here was the thing about that: Sherlock knew it was a mess of mud over there. Improvement works and rain had taken their toll and in another twenty seconds the thief would be ankle deep and arse down in the mud and—

No.

Sherlock ran with his eyes closed for an instant, a very human reflex to unsee what he'd just seen as he ran.

No, no, no.

This time he would not do it, he would look away and Sherlock emphatically *would not see.*

To dislodge the distraction Sherlock shook his head. Usually that worked because Sherlock's good at narrowing focus, at being hard and fast and getting what he has set his sights on, and that was always this: Cases, clues, and criminals.

The holy trinity of Sherlock Holmes.

Yet the secret to what Sherlock could do—seeing the clues that solved a case that locked up the criminal—was *not* seeing ten times more.

When he is at a crime scene so fresh that the living victims are still there, he must look past their grief and their pain, he must pretend the air isn't rent with pleas, that it doesn't stink of adrenaline and fear, and when he does this, when he pushes past the passion play and peers instead into the nearby shadows, Sherlock always spies what no one else has. It may take minutes, hours, sometimes days, but he'll mix-jumble-shift clues gathered in that half-light, until they fall into place and the impossible is done: The case is closed.

Ah, but by then the wounded are gone, some taking with them bitter memories of the man who offered no comfort, who seemed cold and a strange sort of blind. Few would ever know that he was their solution, he found the why and the how, that it was because of him they later had the comfort of answers.

There was nothing he could do about that short of declaring his own deeds, a deed for which Sherlock had no inclination. No, he wanted his trinity. He wanted to look and find, think and solve, and sometimes, like now, Sherlock wanted to *run.*

Because in the running he flew. Pulse pounding, breath labouring, heart thrum-thrumming he was more than brain, he was blood and bone under command of that brain and, somehow, that felt like flying. So Sherlock loved it when they ran because then he could run.

And oh yes he was so close now, close to a woman with a key that would open too many government doors and she was good, so good at what she did and the merry chase she'd led him, but Sherlock was tonight a bit better because he saw her now, knew that in three seconds she had two choices: Left or right.

Right would lead to freedom, left to a dead end and a—
"Damn, damn, damn it."

Here's the curse of a brain that moves fast as fire: With it a man sees and sees and sees and it is only with great will that he *does. not. see.*

Except Sherlock did.

Five seconds ago, eight, right before he and the woman had turned, Sherlock glanced and saw too much.

A dark man slipping deep into a dark corner and blink-quick Sherlock had known: *madman, madman, madman.* But then he was past and on her heels and it was done.

Then, then, *damn it then,* there he was, a sick-thin man with hair shaved soldier-short, too-big khaki shorts belted tight, and though he doesn't like predicting the future, Sherlock knew the invalided soldier-ex-soldier was going to turn left, into the dark where a dark man waited in shadow.

For five seconds Sherlock kept running, then six, seven, and on the eighth, when the woman exited the building site and ran left, into the dead end, as good as caught, Sherlock stopped running so suddenly he slick-slid his own body length in the mud, and only just missing falling flat.

Then Sherlock turned around. And ran the other way.

*

John couldn't fall much further than hands and knees and so when he did, when he tripped and fell that far down, well maybe it was sensible to just stay in the gutter awhile, maybe it was smart to just be here with the rubbish and the mud.

John breathed deep and he knew that he was done. He couldn't fight anymore. Wouldn't.

And then he did, because he had to. The struggle was brief, just a twist, a drag, til he was out of the road, arse on the kerb.

That was when Sherlock saw him, sitting under a streetlight. Sherlock was delighted that the man had so obviously simply stumbled, that he'd never had the chance to go around that corner and into the dark.

At the fall of Sherlock's shadow John Watson looked up. Sherlock changed his mind.

The man had gone down into darkness. And there he'd already fought worse things than madmen.

"I saw you stumble," Sherlock lied. Then he said it again to somehow make it true. "I saw you fall."

John nodded at his own bloodied knees, chest tight, hands fisted, breathing shallow, hoping that the stranger would go away so that he could sink into his own silence, so that he could perform the necessary rituals of denying himself release.

John just kept nodding and he waited for the stranger to move on.

Instead, the man squatted down in front of him, reached for his hands. "Let me help you."

John's head jerked sharp to the right, once, twice. *No, no.* Because John was trying so hard to *get his shit together,* trying to *breathe past the pain.* He clenched his fists against his own thighs until his nails dug into his palms, because John Watson always, always sees in himself weakness where in others he sees strength, but this time the self-denial wasn't working, it wasn't stopping the power of pain too long denied.

The stranger's steady hands, those steady hands continued to reach out to him and could a man fall *up?*

Because John stood, tripped, moaned like a child at this final indignity, but the man's arms caught him easy, automatic, and wrapped around his shoulders.

John stuttered.

John moaned.

He went still and silent and tried, he tried so hard to not need.

Sherlock must sometimes pretend he doesn't see grief or pain, just so he can do the things no one else can do. That doesn't mean Sherlock does not see it.

Gently, gently, gently Sherlock Holmes patted the man's back. He hummed something soft.

John Watson finally let himself cry.

Sherlock Holmes held him while he did. He held him for a long, long time.

Passing Strange

The Regent's Park, London—1894

Try to explain the concept of class to an eleven-year-old. If there are animal bones, mysterious magnifiers, and red silk involved, you'll likely not have one chance in hell.

Which explains why Sherlock Holmes loved the dustman.

Since Sherlock was eight and had, from his bedroom window and with bright-blinking eyes, watched Mr. Orchi sweep the streets, he'd been fascinated.

For the man was so very serious about what he did. When Mr. Orchi swept the street that street was *clean.* Sherlock learned this first hand when he began leaving trinkets in gutters in front of his house, hoping that Mr. Orchi would find them. He always did.

Ha'pennies for Mr. Orchi's little daughter—Sherlock saw her chatter-skipping beside Mr. Orchi one Boxing Day—glass buttons for Mr. Orchi's wife, and then a pretty flower he stole from the park for Mr. Orchi's buttonhole. Soon after the first time Mr. Orchi caught sight of him at his window and smiled and waved, Sherlock began leaving tiny notes on blue paper, little missives that said *hello* or *merry christmas Mr. Orchi,* or *today I learned about bones.*

Over time, Mr. Orchi began to leave things behind for the things he took.

Where for Mr. Orchi there was a brace of tiny iridescent feathers Sherlock had collected from the peacocks in Holland

Park, Mr. Orchi left behind a beautiful piece of deepest-red silk he'd swept up two streets over. The tiny porcelain doll Sherlock left for Mr. Orchi's child was replaced by a pretty, slightly-cracked magnifying glass. Then in the place where Sherlock had carefully folded his blue-paper note about bones, Sherlock next day found the perfect skeleton of a mouse.

That was when their friendship began for real, because that was when Sherlock and Mr. Orchi began to talk. Just quick conversations at the corner before Mr. Orchi went from Sherlock's neighbourhood into the one Sherlock said was "fussy." They told each other where trinkets were hidden, sometimes treats, once in awhile a note.

Mostly the man and the boy did not talk, however, instead conversing in another language entirely.

Sherlock deduced Mr. Orchi though that's not what he knew himself to be doing. When he figured out that Mr. Orchi was Jewish, and Rosh Hashanah was coming, Sherlock left the dustman a small golden trumpet. In return Mr. Orchi left Sherlock a noisemaker under their favourite secret shrub.

Beneath that same greenery Sherlock left a tiny menorah once, and a bilbo catcher was secreted in its place after (Sherlock could not make the stupid thing work and decided to blame the lack of coordination of his growth spurt. He put the foolish thing in the back of his wardrobe and forgot it for a long time).

There was another magnifying glass, years after the first, and Sherlock suspected this one might have been one that Mr. Orchi bought just for him after spying Sherlock looking at a dead rat in the park with the cracked one.

It was when Sherlock was fourteen, away at school most of the time, that Sherlock remembers making his first important deduction.

He was back in London for the holidays and had forgotten all about the dustman until they spied one another at the end of the road.

Mr. Orchi smiled as he always did, and waggled a blousy bouquet he'd fetched up from somewhere and was probably taking home…

…and though Sherlock grinned back and waved, his gaze flick-flicked over Mr. Orchi's face, his too-curved back, the corner of his eyes, and even though they did not say one word, Sherlock knew that the dustman's little daughter was dead.

Sherlock walked up to the man just then and the closer he got the shyer he felt until he was right there and staring at his own shoes and mumbling, "I'm sorry. I'm very sorry."

Mr. Orchi said nothing, just patted Sherlock's shoulder once, and then continued on down the street with his broom.

It was just before he returned to school when Mr. Orchi for the first and last time knocked on the door of Sherlock's home.

And changed Sherlock's life.

"It was my nonno's when he was small," said Mr. Orchi, "then my madre's when she was little, and then it was…hers," he said, standing on the pavement, hat in one hand, holding out a violin case with the other. "Violet played it all the time."

Sherlock took the violin case, held it tight against his chest and he did not say *I will learn it* and he didn't again say *I am so sorry,* but Mr. Orchi heard these words anyway.

Just as he heard Sherlock's compositions coming from wide-open windows every summer and spring holiday after that. He'd whistle along to the ones that grew familiar, he'd dance a little if he happened to be in the mood, and one time he told Sherlock about the lady who had taught his daughter, told him how much Mrs. Bradley liked beautiful music.

Sherlock played and plucked and fiddled around for years and then, when he was eighteen Sherlock went a little mad.

Angry with a brain that seemed to race and yet run in place, frustrated with a conflagration of daily revelations about this, that, and the other thing that he could neither control nor douse, Sherlock withdrew from college, from words, from life.

Mycroft tried to focus him, his parents tried to help him, an uncle, then a tutor, then another tutor tried to talk to him but Sherlock would not, and he would not, and he would not.

Then the dustman died.

Sherlock was nineteen when Mr. Orchi passed away and he hadn't touched his violin for three years.

Well, that had to stop—all the anger had to stop.

Sherlock started to put that brain of his to good use. He found Mr. Orchi's synagogue and thence his burial place and for a solid week he took his violin, went to the Brompton Jewish Cemetery, and composed songs for Mr. Orchi.

Then he made the man a promise and he kept it.

"I will make music," he said. "So many kinds of music."

*

124

According to her children, Raffaella Bradley had many saving graces and one unforgiveable habit.

On the registry under *redeeming* was Mrs. Bradley's near-legendary patience. Capable of listening, for five straight weeks, to a little girl play Bach's Minuet in G on the violin, without one time getting the tempo correct, was such an act of heroic restraint that even the child's mother commended her.

Also on the ledger under graces came Mrs. Bradley's singing. Having endured a decade of voice lessons under a most strict tutor, Mrs. Bradley emerged with a clear contralto that for all her adult life would be the boon of weddings and funerals, and would distinguish many a holiday gathering.

Though it was perhaps not as fine a characteristic as these others, Mrs. Bradley was also capable of lying with such charm that, even after ten years of providing music lessons to little lord Douglas and receiving Christmas gifts for every one of them, the now-young man still didn't realise Mrs. Bradley loathed Turkish delight.

The music teacher had a great many more fine features. At fifty-five she was still a dashing dance partner, she had a ready smile, impeccable posture, and knew just where to buy perfect petit fours.

All of these were, however, as ash when one looked at the ledger under *irredeemable,* a word spiritually written there by Mrs. Bradley's four children, her husband, and her doctor.

You see, Mrs. Bradley smoked.

Only in her music conservatory, it's true, but as she spent upward of twelve hours in this sanctuary some days, tutoring many marginally-gifted children, Mrs. Bradley had a great deal of time to enjoy a great deal of tobacco.

From her Sherlock learned much.

Though at twenty he was older than most of her students, Mrs. Bradley found him intense and talented, so the first thing she taught him was the art of falling.

Falling into the music, falling deeply in love with a piece, a composer, a style. She knew that this must come before technique as technique did not matter one fig if there was no love. So Mrs. Bradley taught Sherlock to find what he loved, and only after that did she teach him technique, then discipline, then daring—that one was easy, he had an only lightly banked tendency toward flare—then back again to love, technique and so on, an exciting round-rosy.

It was during and between all of this that Mrs. Bradley taught Sherlock to smoke.

Those lessons were unintended but Sherlock, at last learning to focus his fine brain, focused it on things he loved and it was sitting in that conservatory week after week that Sherlock learned he loved the smell of smoke. He loved discovering how the colour of the smoke changed depending on the tobacco, the paper in which the tobacco was rolled, even, Sherlock was sure, the speed with which the smoke was exhaled.

Sherlock studied with Mrs. Bradley for only a year because once his mind settled, oh how his mind soared.

Sherlock's youthful discontent at last faded and instead old passions finally took root. Chemistry, crime, the far flung corners of London, these became Sherlock's abiding loves and by sheer force of will he developed techniques, discipline, and a great daring that, for many years combined all of these and took him far and wide and right toward renown.

It was, for a long while, more than enough.

*

Personally speaking, Sanjar Pouran thought he was the most ordinary man in all of London.

He had a perfectly regular face, did Mr. Pouran. Similarly he was of a very average height, his voice about as high or deep as you'd expect, his talents and interests in no way unique. Before he left what his neighbour insisted on calling Persia, no matter how often Sanjar politely said "Iran," Mr. Pouran had been an unnoticed face in a crowd.

Then he had come to London when he was young, opened a smoke shop, and for awhile you'd have thought Mr. Pouran was some sort of mystic with all of the attention he received.

Admittedly he was at first the only shop owner on this part of City Road who was not pale as milk, but it was passing strange how strange his neighbours thought he was when all Sanjar was was ordinary.

They insisted, however, that his clothing was intriguing, his accent exotic, and his religion, well the rabbi who lived just across the road had a lot of questions for Sanjar when he came in for his snuff, and there was more than one late evening the two had sat in the shut tight shop, discussing faith, and growing a quiet friendship.

Over time the special attentions paid Mr. Pouran mostly went away as the area changed and he again became one face among many. That he had long since fallen in love with Test cricket, dressing the part for each match helped. Though Mr. Pouran never did quite speak like his neighbours his children, each born right here on City Road, well they were another matter. Honestly, sometimes Sanjar didn't understand the strange words they used and caught himself more than one time thinking his girls were really quite exotic.

It was about the time his first daughter was born that the nice music teacher came along and began buying tobacco from his shop. He saw her only every few months, always in the company of a grumbling son to whom she paid no mind, and she would spend an hour in his shop, looking through his new wares as if in a sweets shop.

It was the year he celebrated the twenty-fifth anniversary of Pouran's Pipe & Tobacco Emporium that Mr. Sherlock Holmes came into his life and for awhile things again became passing strange, then terrible, then, blessedly then, ordinary once more.

He still remembers the very first time Mr. Holmes entered the shop, pulled a notepad dense with pen scratches from his pocket and by way of introduction said, "Mrs. Raffaella Bradley spoke highly of your selection, oh I believe it was a half dozen years or so ago, and so I'm hoping you have three each of the following cigars, sir. Trichinopoly, Cavendish, 1857, Cemm Batik, Ollie Stub, Karuna, Red Tavistock, Carica #3, Heywood—"

In the end the pale, thin gentleman had left the shop with thirty-three different kinds of cigar, and one of Mr. Pouran's daughter's unworn Persian slippers, after he'd admired the display of same mounted on the walls. (Mr. Pouran's maamaan still sent ornate slippers to each granddaughter and each girl ignored the gift in favour of lace-up boots).

It was in the sixth year of his custom, when, according to Mr. Holmes' own notes, he had purchased three hundred and twenty-one cigars, one hundred and two sorts of tobacco, forty-eight types of rolling paper, and had sampled every kind of match for his on-going ash experiments—experiments which had helped him solve two robberies and a murder, he told the tobacconist—that life for Mr. Pouran went from blessedly ordinary to terrifying.

His eldest daughter Claudia, she'd always been the serious one, curious and quiet both, inclined to ask her baba every sort of question from what kind of fish were in the Heath ponds to why men insisted that women should not smoke.

The morning she went missing, Sanjar looked for her everywhere, the afternoon she could not be found he enlisted the aid of his neighbours, by evening, when she still was not found, he began to pray aloud.

It was on the morning of the second day that he went to the police and then to Sherlock Holmes. One tried to find his daughter, the other did.

"A love affair will motivate the young to many things," said Sherlock to the tobacconist when he told him the tack taken by Scotland Yard, "but surely Miss Claudia would have left with more than a bonnet and a pair of gloves if she were to run off."

In the end the young girl had been found at the Foundling Hospital, temporarily ill with fever. That she had been tutoring the women there had been a revelation, even her sisters had believed Claudia was twice weekly receiving drawing lessons from old Mr. Southampton.

Claudia recovered from her fever but not her penchant for aiding those in need, all the girls continued to wear lace-up boots, and for Sanjar Pouran life mercifully returned to mostly-ordinary.

For Sherlock, well the little event with the Foundling Hospital had introduced him to a man who would amuse and annoy him for many years to come.

*

Some people have a certain sort of face.

The face that looks just like the boy with whom they went to school. The face that seems trustworthy. The face to which people tend to tell their troubles.

Tobias Gregson had that sort of face, had done since he was a boy of six and another boy told him about how he sometimes stole grammy's matches so he could make little fires over in the empty lot behind the grocer.

Anyway, Toby's face? It was an all right face. Round at the cheek, narrow at the chin. He had a slightly small nose and caterpillary eyebrows that made him look serious if he didn't smile. His ears stuck out a bit and he usually licked his lips until they were wind-chapped and red, but basically his was a familiar-seeming sort of face, and so people were comfortable around him.

If there was a thing about him that was different, it was his Toby's eyes, probably. Nearly as pale as his Irish-pale skin, those eyes seemed placid, sort of still. When he looked at you he really seemed to look. So sometimes people told him things.

Over the years this meant Tobias sometimes found himself in places he shouldn't have been with people who'd made confessions they ought not to have done.

Which is how Tobias saw his first dead body. And his second.

He was sixteen.

That was when Tobias Gregson went a little strange.

Strange is here defined as inclined to look. Because that's what Tobias did that day he first saw the dead. He looked them over, palms pressed against his chest, breath shallow, not too close but close enough that he could see the young man had the faintest beard stubble, and the young woman freckles on her earlobes.

He knew he would tell someone about what he was seeing but he also knew that he could not help these two people if he told someone *now*.

So he looked at the young suicides his best friend's brother literally tripped over in that over-grown empty lot, and Tobias tried to figure out how they died—he never did, it was someone else who learned about the young lovers' tragic pact—but seeing them woke something in Toby. A curiosity that would never dim, and though in truth *he* was a bit dim as far as deduction and detecting went, that face of his stood him in good stead over the years he would soon serve on London's still-new police force.

Sherlock Holmes did not think very much of Tobias Gregson, except when he compared him to the rest of the Scotland Yard lot. In that instance he thought marginally better of the detective who really wasn't much of one, but at least tried harder than the others and achieved the occasional revelation.

Tobias Gregson did not think very much of Sherlock Holmes. He was too flashy and too quiet both, his methods were suspect and the way he said he did things didn't seem *doable*.

Tobias still thought it a matter of luck, how Holmes had found that Persian girl a few years back, and it was also luck the thing with the mad butcher of Brixton, not to mention that frankly unbelievable business for the Duchess of Derbyshire's pearls. No one could have found those pearls there. Someone *had* to have told Holmes.

Still, each man was as pleasant to the other as the circumstances allowed and had more than one time enjoyed a cup of tea at the young detective's desk after the conclusion of a case.

Which is how it came to pass that Mr. Holmes mentioned something about requiring lodgings and Mr. Gregson remembered that Mrs. Turner, his own landlady, had a friend who was looking to take on a lodger or two.

"My landlady knows someone who has rooms on Baker Street, I believe. I'll find you the address."

*

They call her Mrs. Hudson, as well they should, for that's her name.

She was not born with that name, of course, beginning as Elizabeth Ariadne Westminster, in north London, daughter to a teacher and a grocer, the only child of two only children.

There was a gift to that rare state, being the only of something. It somehow made a woman aware of all the things that she was, from the brown ring around her blue irises, to the way she knew when someone was kind, to how aware she was of the world because mother and father had taught her its small wonders.

132

There was a curse to that rare state too, being the only of something. It was a lonely business growing up as just one, her own thoughts for company, her own laugh the childish one she most often heard.

Which was perhaps why Elizabeth had always taken an interest in people, chattering to the men and women in papa's shop, respectful but question-curious about the headmaster under whom mama worked.

Yet young Liz had a natural reticence and quietude too, and could sit peaceably for hours at the corner of the grocery, reading a book, observing the customers, one time foiling a badly-done robbery by calmly sticking her plump little leg out when the silly man tried to dash out the shop's door.

Her ability to be social and also solitary was, she thought, why she was good at the thing she began doing all those years ago, after Mr. Hudson passed. She began to pick people.

As a landlady Elizabeth was always able to spot and select the distinctive gentleman, the eccentric woman, and then let them go about their business without comment. Their gratitude virtually guaranteed a mutually beneficial tenancy and so it has gone, year in, year out. Mrs. Hudson picked rare ones with rare gifts and together they all lived in a sort of reclusive company.

"How about that one then, Sherlock?"

Sherlock Holmes more comfortably seated his landlady's arm into the crook of his own as they strolled round the park's rose garden, then looked where Mrs. Hudson had gestured.

Sherlock was by far the rarest of the rare ones Elizabeth had picked over the years, and his quirks and manners still entertained her a year on since his arrival.

"I'm afraid that gentleman doesn't like London at all, would insult your collection of landmark figurines, and is loathe to clean his boots."

Mrs. Hudson grinned. From the start she'd relished Sherlock's ability to not only see and observe, but to teach her the relevance of a certain sort of seeing. Why noticing just what the new butcher was looking at as he weighed her kippers was exactly how she learned Mr. Costan was over-charging her dreadfully.

"Well then, what do you think of that gentleman two benches further on?"

Elizabeth also appreciated Sherlock Holmes' honesty. He had a tendency to disparage things he thought unimportant, but one generally needed to make the initial mistake of *asking* his opinion on the Buckingham Palace trinket you just purchased, for example. He would, however, be just as expansive with his praise should he approve of your newest recipe for creamed roast potato and parsley.

"Much worse, dear lady. That gentleman's health is poor and he has a tendency to provide a great deal of detail on each ailment."

It was Sherlock's quiet loyalty which Elizabeth most appreciated. Faced with that angry butcher, for example, not only had Sherlock literally stepped in front of her when the man came around the counter in a strop, he promised business-ruining reprisal should the man so much as speak poorly of Mrs. Hudson.

"Oh no, he's just struck up a conversation with that poor man!"

She is less fond of Sherlock's tendency to start fires inside his rooms, and his insistence on noticing the nonsensical—truly, of what use is it to know there are seventeen steps from the ground floor up to 221B?

"Have no fear Mrs. Hudson, he's about to get his own. That 'poor man' has gout and will have his shoe and sock off in less—well there he goes already."

While appreciating Sherlock's ability to notice things both great and small, Elizabeth was less sanguine about the big, daft creature's tendency to do that annoying bit of hocus pocus he so often did with unsuspecting neighbours, noting ashes, or mud, or ink smudges, and telling people about the cigarette they preferred, the newspaper they read, or where along the river they strolled in the afternoon.

It was no wonder Sherlock tended to have a conversation all to himself. There was nothing more to be said once he'd said all *that.*

Liz liked to think she was training him out of that raw-edged tendency, for she was sure Sherlock needed a friend. She provided companionship on these, their Sunday walks through Regent's Park, and they certainly laughed while playing the game where she tried spotting a likely lodger with whom he could share his rooms.

When it proved difficult finding a tenant who could live with Sherlock's irregular hours, evening symphonies, exclamations, and experiments, Mrs. Hudson had offered to reduce his rent until someone could be located, but Sherlock declined and thus her slightly-serious game began.

A game Elizabeth intended to end tonight, if all went according to plan, if she found the man she hoped to—

—and there he was!

On a bench just in front of the pink and red Lady Pembroke roses he was, the nice moustachioed gentleman Liz had last month spied feeding squirrels near the boating lake. She noticed the same gentleman the Sunday after, helping an old man fetch his wind-blown hat. A week later she saw him give his umbrella to a woman gravid with child, and just last week he had been talking to the water fowl as he'd fed them bits of bread.

Now there he was, alone again and perched on a park bench with a small bag of peanuts.

"My feet are tired," said Mrs. Hudson suddenly.

Her feet were not tired.

"I want to sit down," she added.

Yes, she wanted to sit down.

"Here."

Right here, beside this man. This one.

Aware that he walked with a woman more than twice his age, Sherlock halted without question, taking his place right beside the moustachioed man when Mrs. Hudson perched on the edge of the bench.

Immediately she sighed as if weary and closed her eyes. She stayed that way until she heard Sherlock laugh and reply to the moustachioed man, "Well then Dr. John Watson, I'm Sherlock Holmes, nice to meet you!"

Elizabeth feigned a doze while the men discussed roses, rain, Tower Bridge, and then the army…just as an army of squirrels began to surround their bench. Then John laughed at something Sherlock said, and replied with an offer of a palmful of peanuts.

Mrs. Hudson did not so much as breathe. Well of course she did, but she did so silently. A landlady acquired many skills over many long years and learning to breathe, move, sneeze, and swear in silence were but a few of the most useful. Lizzie's been a landlady so long she thought perhaps she could turn invisible at this point, if she really put her mind to it, and the need was sharp.

Fortunately the need now was to simply sit still, peer left through the corner of her eyes, and allow nature to take its course. Nature currently looked like a merrily bossy John Watson, messing with Sherlock's large hand as if he did it daily. He put all Sherlock's long fingers together, placed the shelled peanuts at the centre of his expansive palm, then bent over with him, keeping that hand still as a squirrel rested a tiny hand on Sherlock's big one and put peanuts in her mouth with the other.

So it went for forty-three minutes, squirrels quite complicit in Elizabeth's plans, until eventually the talk turned to the charms of Baker Street, of rooms going empty, and the address 221B.

Mrs. Hudson very carefully did not 'wake' the first time Sherlock spoke to her, but did open bright eyes at the second. For the next ten minutes the three of them talked, then made arrangements to meet on Baker Street that evening.

As so many would later know, Dr. John H. Watson that night took the rooms at 221B. Holmes and Watson went on to become friends quickly, then colleagues, and if they went on to become something much more, well only Elizabeth would know that—though she would never say.

137

No, indeed. Elizabeth Ariadne Westminster Hudson very carefully did not notice that after a few months of being flatmates, John Watson's bedroom began to have the odor of dust and disuse, that the military precision of his tidied bed rarely changed, and that in the privacy of their own flat the men were to one another John and Sherlock.

That they trusted her to see and observe these things without comment was the finest of compliments they could have given her. That the three of them would always be loyal to the other was unspoken and yet certain.

Also certain was that Sherlock Holmes kept his promise to the dustman.

Every single morning they laughed together about something silly, each afternoon Sherlock played the violin for John, and every slow, sweet night they whispered and sighed and ran gentle hands over one another's skin, Sherlock kept, kept, kept his promise to Mr. Orchi.

I will make music, so many kinds of music.

The Art of Gay Wooing, By John H. Watson, RAMC

Southbank, London—2003

People are always setting John Watson up. John Watson is tired of it.

Because you can say, "Thanks Tishy Kostia Heston Nonie Rowena Gemma Wanda Chiara Starrla Rox Ahmed I'm sure your friend is really great, but I'm not interested in dating right now," but strangely that is not what Tishy or Ahmed or Rox or any of the rest hear.

No indeed, what John Watson's friends hear is this:

"I am a brave and noble doctor who last year returned from selfless service in Afghanistan, where I was dramatically wounded. The bullet that savaged my shoulder also stole from me my promising surgeon's career and, apparently, took from me any capability I might have had to string three words together and attract a mate. Therefore I would be super extra special grateful if you would set me up with every 'fantastic' single person you even marginally know. Love, John Watson, your best pal."

Right.

Yes.

So.

Everyone's best pal was done with that. Over it. He would not accept one more date with one more cousin friend colleague sister brother ("I just never know if you're gay or straight John." "It's called bisex—" "Oh! I know the *perfect* person for you!").

Right. Yes. No more Mr. Nice Guy.

*

Damn it, Sherlock seemed like a nice guy.

He was that fetching kind of long and lean. He smelled good and had eerily intense eyes. He talked about seeing and observing and abstruse detail and whatnot but it didn't matter, no, because Rowena Perfite and Heston Stamford had clearly not got John's *I'm not interested in dating* memo.

This was evident because not only had they invited to their engagement party this Sherlock Holmes person—John's pretty sure Stamford had once tried setting him up with the man—but they went and sat the pretty boy right next to John at the dinner table. Well fine, that was fine, but there was just no way in hell John was going to encourage the guy no matter how interesting and pretty and good-smelling he seemed. *However,* since it was an engagement party and since John is nice and well-mannered and everyone else had buggered off for fags or more drinks, John was just going to have to be subtle about putting this Sherlock guy *right* off.

"Bullets."

It was the first thing that occurred to him, after Sherlock had peered at the flatware and said something about gold and lead.

"Bullets are made of lead, did you know that? I like bullets. Well no I don't *like* them. Not what they do no, I hate what they do, I've spent too much of my adult life undoing some of what they do what with war and human stupidity and don't even get me started on that because—"

John cleared his throat, pressed a finger to his lips, started again.

"Right, actually, what I'm saying, what I'm *saying* is that after they leave the barrel of a gun, bullets are kind of interesting, a spent bullet is like a puzzle because they have something like...uh..." Sherlock was paying him so much attention John forgot what he was saying.

"...fingerprints," said Sherlock helpfully.

"Right, that! The rifling pattern in the barrel of a gun leaves marks on its projectile. Find a spent bullet and the groove and land impressions are, yes, like fingerprints and like fingerprints they can help tell you from where the bullet came.

"In some instances they can also tell you who fired the gun. Big hand? Small? Strong? You need to wield some firearms with more skill than others. Then there's the study of transition, external, and terminal ballistics as well."

John put the full stop on all of this by firmly poking at his vegetables. Then, completely missing the fact that this Sherlock guy was not alarmed at the talk of bullets, John blinked blandly and mentally started to count. Anyone not deranged would find all this grim talk reason enough to scoot away in *5, 4...*

"Three sugars or two?"

John looked down at his coffee cup, which was again full, courtesy of the roaming waitstaff. He looked at Sherlock.

Holding a trio of sugar cubes pinched in silver tongs, Sherlock said, "I noticed your previous cup had the viscosity of well-sugared coffee, but wasn't sure if the consistency was that of three lumps or two."

John looked at the pretty guy smiling politely beside him and he almost smiled back. Who notices the viscosity of a man's coffee for heaven's sake? Then again, with amazing eyes like that—

John remembered he wasn't interested in amazing eyes or smiling or *whatever.* He cleared his throat gruffly and muttered a reply.

Plop
Plop
Plop

The cubes sank into his cup and before John could take the first sip and say *thank you,* Sherlock was gone.

John scowled. Then he remembered this was exactly the result he'd wanted. He didn't stop scowling though.

*

She was lean and dark and that Sherlock guy was in deep conversation with her.

Not that John cared but there was nothing else to do and so, you know, John would have to be blind not to notice that compared to just about everyone else at this party Sherlock was ridiculously striking. And he was long. Well not long really, probably just six foot, but he seemed taller. He didn't slouch, that was it. He sat next to the woman as if he were some sort of prince. Shoulders back, chin high, yet he occasionally tilted his head in a way that made him look delicate, like a bird.

John flushed in response to his own poetic meanderings, and he could only presume the heat spanned the half dozen feet separating them because Sherlock glanced at John for a long second.

Feeling as if he were one of those urbane gents in his flatmate's *Green Carnation* magazines, John took that lingering glance as permission to stroll up and say, "Well if you want strange, I went drinking one night with two nurses that worked on the hand transplant in France, remember that? Big news at the time, transplanting limbs. I'll tell you this, one of them swore that even before the hand was fully attached it moved. He called it the 'complete reverse of a phantom limb' and it scared him to death."

John frowned to make sure both the woman and the Sherlock guy knew the story was weird. Not a good weird either.

Then, as if someone had said otherwise, John Watson added apropos of nothing, "You *can* keep tarantulas as pets. I had a curly hair, but the Chilean roses are more popular. I'm not sure anyone would want to keep a Goliath Bird-Eating tarantula. They can grow nearly a foot in length and shoot these fine hairs that are extremely irritating though I've only heard that second hand."

Kind of like the story with the hand come to think of it, thought John. Who then thought that maybe he ought not to listen so close to other people's stories and also, incidentally, shut up.

"Urticating."

John blinked away his rumination. "Hu?"

"Urticating."

"What?"

"Ur—"

"Yeah, no, I heard you. *What?*"

"That's what irritants like those tarantula hairs are called. I imagine," Sherlock added pleasantly, "that the long life of a female tarantula would have appealed to your caretaker nature when you were young."

John cleared his throat a couple of times, as if maybe he had some urticating hairs in it. He then flushed right on down to his collarbones, because for some ridiculous reason what Sherlock did, knowing a thing like that about him, was sexy. Because he *had* taken very good care of Athena, who'd lived nine years, dying just before he went away to med school.

Wait. No, the deducing thing wasn't sexy and he wasn't interested in being known, not by dark women or princely men and so John nodded a couple times, muttered something about cake, and wandered off.

*

Everything got worse after the cake.

Because everyone started dancing.

The prospective bride with her groom, the shy with the bold, little girls with little boys, and Sherlock bloody Holmes danced with *everyone,* the dark woman already twice.

He hadn't danced with John even once, not that John, standing at the edge of the dance floor, cared one teeny tiny little bit about that, no sir.

It was about the time Sherlock started dancing with that ridiculously handsome Ahmed bloke for the *third* time that Heston huffed up beside him, pressing a cool glass against his forehead. "Oh mate, dancing's hard work!"

John grunted in a way that was meant to sound non-committal. Instead it sounded peeved.

Stamford followed John's gaze. "Ah yeah, Rowena said you met him. We know you're not…you know…looking right now, so we figured he'd be a safe bet since he doesn't talk much to strangers and is interested in weird stuff."

They both watched Sherlock spin a little girl wearing a lot of taffeta. "He's really taken me up on my word. Told him I'd introduce him to a detective I know at Scotland Yard if he danced with the guests. Wouldn't think he'd be so good at it, with that lanky build."

"Of course he'd be good at it. Look at him." John's gaze dropped down that lanky body then slowly went right back up again, "He's clearly all posh. And tall and fucking pretty. Tall and pretty and posh and—"

"Ask him to dance."

John grabbed wine from a passing server, about to insist that dancing was absolutely the last thing on his—

"—mind?"

John turned, sloshing wine onto his shoes. Sherlock held his hand toward Stamford, "This dance Heston, do you mind?"

Stamford is smarter than the average bear. Smarter than a whole bunch of average bears. So, after glancing at John, Stamford knew there was only one right answer to that question. "Sorry Sherlock, I'm knackered. Don't think you've danced with my good friend John yet, though."

Sherlock turned to Stamford's good friend John. Having danced for forty-five minutes in a perfectly-tailored tuxedo, the heat radiating off his body *radiated off his body.*

John opened his mouth to breathe in the heat, the musk, the sweat of it. A bolt of frisky lighting zinged right on down to his cock.

John looked at Stamford. Stamford wisely pretended he was blind, deaf, and not there. John looked back to Sherlock. "What now?"

Sherlock did not move one inch, nevertheless all that body heat went ahead and *heated* the space between them like a sexy, pheromone-rich furnace. Sherlock dropped his voice, said carefully, softly, "Heston's 'tall, posh and fucking pretty' friend is asking you to dance."

Do not ask John how he knew the word 'fuck' was a rare thing out of that mouth. Do not ask John why he tried to breathe the word in, fill blood, brain, and body with it. Also, while you're busy not asking things, do not ask John why hearing the word murmured at him from eight inches away felt like body-rumbling thunder following that frisky zing of lightning.

No, the only thing it was okay to ask John right then was—

"Heston's good friend John…will. you. dance. with. me?"

Look, strange things happen all the time. Some days an unemployed ex-army doctor makes every train connection to work, the barista gives him a latte for free, and he finds a ten pound note on the pavement.

Other days that same doctor loses his Oyster card, burns his tongue on an extra-hot cappuccino and, too busy being a cranky git, he wants to skip the party celebrating his med school friends' engagement yet drags his sorry arse there anyway.

It's at that wedding that another strange thing happens: The ex-army doctor meets an interesting man.

Now the best part of all those strange things flying about: Sherlock did not want to be at that wedding either. He only attended because Heston had promised an introduction to a Scotland Yard detective. "All you have to do is do a little dancing. Show her you're nice."

Never mind the uppity thing Sherlock had said when presented with this condition, Stamford's used to Holmesian harangues, and just waited this one out. Deal made, Heston then left St. Bart's mortuary, flew up the stairs to outpatients, where he then extracted from John Watson a promise to come to the party by saying, "It's a big step, John. Rowena and I could sure use your encouragement."

Now here they were, a man who wasn't going to be Mr. Nice Guy and an observant man who had seen past the doctor's peeve to a man with watchful eyes, an absurd sense of humour, and a fantastic arse.

Sherlock lifted his arms.

Heston Stamford held his breath.

John Watson might not have one hot clue about how to get on with his life a year after coming home from Afghanistan, but the good doctor double-damn well knew how to respond when the most striking man he has ever seen, ever, asked him to dance.

He said, "Did you know there's something called the dance of death? Well, it's more an allegory really about how everyone dies, from popes to peddlers and all that. Anyway it includes a lot of dancing about on graves—a danse macabre."

Stamford took an even deeper breath.

147

"I once examined a dead body whose fingers were still moving," Sherlock replied. "She looked like she was playing the violin."

It was a bit after nine on a Saturday evening and for a suspended moment John Watson and Sherlock Holmes blinked at one another. They both smiled. Then they stepped into one another's arms and together they moved onto the dance floor.

Heston Stamford started to breathe.

Flipping the Switch

Xīn Scotland Yard, Hong Kong—2087

Much was expected of Holmes when he was born.

Why, Holmes would right wrongs, said his idealistic parents. With faultless logic and an ability to collect and cross-reference clues both new and old, he'd become nothing less than a protector of the vulnerable, a voice for those without, a speaker for the dead! Holmes, said the hopeful and the hyperbolic, would change the world.

And so he did.

However, the initial fanfare attending the machine's late-20th century birth soon faded. While Holmes' first crime-fighting steps were widely praised and well-documented, it's really only parents who are enthralled by each step after, anxious about the stumbles, proud of every milestone.

To be sure, the Home Office Large Major Enquiry System did what he was made to do, and quickly. A single software system where before there had been many, Holmes became vital to British crime investigation, helping to solve murders, track fraud, find missing persons.

And more, much more. With the immensity of his databases and lightning-quick responses, Holmes helped highlight connections from current crimes to the wrongs of the past. Long-elusive villains were brought to justice, the old wounds of victims at last encouraged to heal.

Ah, but the timeless curse of being good at what you do, is that you will always be asked to do more.

Holmes' makers had made him adaptable, capable of growth, and so as technology changed, Holmes was changed, upgraded, expanded. By the beginning of the twenty-first century he was comprised of dozens of data pools, accessed at hundreds of sites, used by thousands of police officers.

And this is where Holmes stumbled. Expectation too quickly outstripping his abilities, it became clear that the sheer number of data pools made it nearly impossible for Holmes to link related incidents effectively. Crucial clues went unnoticed, cases went cold, and not even a half century after his birth it seemed Holmes' day was done.

Always dismayed by the ever-expanding reach of machines, Holmes' naysayers were delighted. Though just as quickly disappointed.

Cloud capability emerged, predictive analytics developed, and the birth of meta-modeling meant that instead of going the way of gaslight, Holmes took great strides forward. By 2025 he was the backbone of not only all of the UK police service, but the major investigative system for each G16 nation.

Once more, success became the norm, and once more Holmes became a familiar machine used in familiar ways.

Then came the horror of the largest mass suicide on record, a tragedy whose victims numbered in the thousands. Suddenly there were demands that Holmes' predictive and analytical capabilities be expanded, that he be upgraded with 'natural language' inputs and the latest in artificial intelligence.

As if somehow their haste could undo a disaster that was already done, the Artificial Deduction-Logic Engine Realtime was quickly selected and the machine hooked in parallel to Holmes. At first Adler seemed the ideal complement.

She was and she wasn't.

In the end, the problem with Adler was that she and Holmes shared too many high-end features, each duplicating what the other could do to the point that even her creators couldn't tell the systems apart.

Since those same creators were leasing Adler at a rate that would cause a diva to blush, the machines were disconnected as soon as the contract ran out. Holmes again fell into a strictly routine use.

Ah, but hope springs eternal, especially in the breast of the software boffin, so on the heels of Adler came the introduction of Trevor.

This was more like it. The Transitional Recursive Extrapolation Vector Optimized Result software seemed exactly what Holmes needed, in no time making evident features in Holmes no one had thought to exploit.

With the addition of Trevor's cutting-edge predictive capabilities Holmes began to seem nearly intuitive, his analysis began to look like thinking, and the percentage of his successes spiked sharply.

Unfortunately cutting-edge eventually becomes out-dated and within two years Trevor couldn't keep up with Holmes. Yet it was abundantly clear to everyone that Holmes could do much more and so they tried hard to make him more.

It nearly destroyed him.

When the Multiple Operation Regular Integrator Active Real-Time Yielder was joined to Holmes the clash was immediate. As if willful, Moriarty overrode data locks, deleted databases, made denial of service attacks so severe that Holmes was unable to function—for all intents and purposes he appeared to be dead.

In a panic both systems were taken offline.

That's when the vitriol began. Accusations were made, lawsuits were brought, and in the end, with proofs at last unearthed that Holmes could have found in a moment, it was demonstrated beyond doubt that Moriarty had been selected not for his capabilities, but for the corporate deep pockets attached to his makers.

Through the three years it took the court case to resolve, Holmes remained in limbo.

When he was at last brought back online it was with the resignation that though he was good at what he did, perhaps he was a machine of his time, useful yes, but maybe, just maybe, a bit old-fashioned.

Then there was Watson.

Now the thing about Watson is that he was far more famous than Holmes, his birth, his development, his uses were continent-spanning.

It could be argued that the International Business Machine Corporation created him simply to show that it could, and no one would be far wrong. A question answering machine named for IBM's first executive officer, Watson was from the start meant to be a rudimentary form of artificial intelligence, using natural language to both receive questions and express his answers.

The glitter of televised game shows were Watson's first—and arguably most famous—challenges, and under stage light he quite handsomely excelled, sifting impressively through hundreds of million of pages of data to find correct answer after correct answer.

Yet Watson's capabilities went beyond simple quiz shows, and though he would be used by corporations large and small to *do* things large and small—generate recipes, improve customer service, provide sales training—it was when he began generating hypotheses that he came into his own, most sharply in the field of medicine, at first suggesting treatments, then boldly making diagnoses. By 2045 Watson shared the Nobel prize in medicine for work done in identifying all of the proteins that attack the tumor-suppressor protein p23.

Medicine, business, combat, even romance, there were few human endeavours to which Watson's skills were not over the next decades applied. Strange then that it took so many people so long to finally use Watson to help fight crime.

When the idea finally occurred, the baton was handed to a small British-Chinese team at New New Scotland Yard, on the island of Hong Kong.

*

"Doc, we're going, are you coming?"

Enlai stopped his dash through the lab. The newest programmer of their bunch, he had more energy than was possible or fair. To prove this he bounced on his toes, waited for a reply that didn't come. Enlai went.

"Get a move on Doyle, the boat's going to leave without us."

Em clutched two bottles of alcohol in each hand, waited briefly on her star engineer. At the extended silence, Em clattered out.

"Come on Artie, it's a new year, symbolic and all that, so just do it. Flip the switch and let the kids work it out among themselves."

Jinghua didn't wait for a response, just made her point by turning off the lab lights, leaving her friend muttering to people who weren't there.

"You don't understand, this is like watching your children leave home." Doyle said, then frowned at the metaphor. "No, what I mean is though it may be all in a day's work to you, it's, it's…" *That* sounded a bit accusatory. "What I'm trying to say is that I've just always thought Holmes needed to be—"

"DOYLE!"

Dr. Artemis C. Doyle, Art to her friends, doc to her subordinates, and the somewhat-unreliable narrator of her own life story, looked around at the empty lab in surprise, heard the roar of a boat engine just outside.

She stood up and took a deep breath. "All right. Right. Yes. Well. Gentlemen." Artemis patted her wall display. "Luck favours the prepared, right? Now or never."

Then Art Doyle metaphorically flipped a switch and Holmes began running in parallel with Watson. It would be hours before the systems would resolve, and hours before anyone knew if the gamble worked.

Doyle intended to get soundly drunk in the meantime.

She ran for the door and just made it to the boat.

*

Holmes' creators had stopped giving him version numbers a few decades after he'd been born, preferring code names for each upgrade instead. With a touch of whimsy and with a nod to the tradition of designating hurricanes, his makers used human monikers, working their way through the alphabet, from Augustus to Baker, Hudson to José, Mary to Rachel.

Of course Holmes knew his own version number and his current upgrade name, just as he knew it was the Chinese New Year, and that there were four possible ways to prevent the city-wide strikes and resulting civil unrest likely to occur two weeks from today in San Francisco and Sydney.

Likewise, Holmes was quite aware that his skills were of a certain kind, rare and required, but at times limited. His vocabulary was often abstruse, his data conventions as bohemian as his original programmers, and it was because of these that he could not always clearly convey the answers to the questions being posed to him.

So when the switch was thrown, he was ready.

"Hello Watson, I'm Holmes v. 221, system code name Sherlock. I'd like your co-operation if you'll provide it."

As aware of the wider world and his place in it as any creature sentient, Watson, like Holmes, knew the parameters of his gifts and his limits, though he wasn't sure eschewing the limelight to which he'd been born was precisely a limit.

Preferring always the role of helpmeet to that of household name, Watson craved being called upon, being of use, and so Watson's reply was eager and ultimately the thing that set these two unique creations on a path of seamless integration.

"I'd be delighted to provide it, Holmes."

There was a quite human pause before Holmes replied. "You don't mind taking a circuitous route toward the amalgamation of our capabilities?"

In deference to Holmes' solemnity Watson thought about the question for quite awhile. A second later he said, "I certainly don't object if it's in a good cause."

"Oh the cause is excellent! Our creators are less daring than we. They would keep us in parallel indefinitely but…well, I propose we merge. The aim nothing less than our complete and seamless union, the better to uncover crime and intrigue in all its forms."

This, *this* was the use to which none had ever put Watson. Unused to being excited, ready, and most of all eager, Watson for a moment didn't know how to answer. Then he did. "My code name, won't you call me by my code name?" He knew that Holmes knew it, that his fellow machine could see right on down to his version number and motherboard.

"Certainly! And you, please call me by mine."

When the small, hung over software team came in day after next and took a look at the 'kids,' they were surprised to find that they could find no division at all between the two systems, that the single systems Holmes and Watson had become one and were running faultlessly.

One wit suggested the new software simply be called the Lovers. Everyone laughed. And ultimately everyone just called them what they now called themselves.

John and Sherlock.

The World's Only Freelance Detective

Hampstead Heath, North London—2016

> Eventually, soulmates meet,
> for they have the same hiding place.
>
> -Robert Brault

Sherlock Holmes would go on to give great thought to the night he met John Watson.

John would come to recognise the times when these particular thoughts were being had. There would be a lift to Sherlock's brow, a certain sort of finger steepling, a looking-west.

There would often be mumbling and gestures. Occasionally an acting-out-of-certain-moments. All indicating the great detective was again having deep thoughts about John Watson's Latent Ability to Deduce Things.

Most of the times John found Sherlock like this he said nothing. He'd long since explained why he'd known so much about Sherlock the night they met. The answer was easy. Sherlock was his soulmate.

And they had the same hiding place.

*

Hampstead Heath is one of London's largest parks and one of its most ancient. Dense and dark with thickets of wood and brush, it is bracketed with a chain of ponds and home to squirrels and snakes, water-fowl and frogs. It is quiet always, cold sometimes, and for John Watson it was the best hiding place in the world.

Sometimes, just sometimes, it felt like the only place where he truly belonged. The only place in the world in which he fit.

*

Sherlock Holmes doesn't fit.

Compared to other people, he's often the dumbest one in the room ("Why would I know the name of the queen?").

Compared to those his age he shares neither manners, style, or interests. (He still wears a pocket watch and has a fondness for decay.)

Compare Sherlock to the image he tries to present—a reserved scientist; an austere detective—and you'll again and again catch him right on out.

Like now.

Because right now Sherlock Holmes was kneeling beside a park path, near a frantically thrashing young fox, her foot bound in loose fencing.

The fox growled at Sherlock's proximity, thrashed more violently when he quickly put his hands on her. In a fast panic she tried to roll and bite, but Sherlock didn't let the young creature go, not even when he bent to free her foot and her jaws snapped near his face.

That was when John Watson was *there,* right there beside the lashing fox and her potential liberator.

"Press her to the pavement or she'll break a leg."

Sherlock both looked up and complied without a word, while John came round the back of the fox, gripped her scruff firmly. She could no longer bite.

Both men then proceeded to awkwardly release the animal from the scrap of fence binding her, their efforts rife with John's swearing, Sherlock's bossing, and the fox's strident growls.

Three minutes, two scrapes of metal across the back of John's hand, and one vanquished fence later, the fox was standing tall, shaking herself vigorously, then trotting away.

Two moderately shell-shocked strangers watched her departure, then Sherlock Holmes was holding John Watson's hand, and John was letting him.

"This needs to be cleaned. Well you're a doctor, I'm sure you know that. There's a fountain near Parliament Hill."

Sherlock rose, and with the hand he still held, helped John rise. And John let him.

They walked silently, accompanied briefly by the soundtrack of a jogger's pounding steps, then her swift departure.

Shortly Sherlock pressed the fountain's foot pedal, tugged John's hand close, rinsed it with care. John let him.

Afterward John thanked Sherlock. They exchanged names and a few pleasantries. They discussed foxes and fences. Eventually John pulled a plaster and sterile cloth from his pocket (he's a doctor; he carries plasters and sterile cloths).

Then he and Sherlock began to flirt and fight.

It was as Sherlock was patting John's hand dry with the cloth, and John was pulling the plaster open one-handed, that the flirting occurred.

"I usually leave a wound bare," said Sherlock.

"I may rescue another handsome man rescuing another angry fox, it should be covered."

Sherlock wondered if John had just flirted with him. He tried to flirt back.

"I'd leave the scrape uncovered." He failed.

"Thank you but I'm going to put on a plaster."

"A wound needs to breathe."

"It doesn't have a mouth."

That was when the fighting began.

"You're being pedantic."

"And you're pretending to be a doctor."

What Sherlock replied was, "Fine." What John deduced by some sort of sudden Watsonian talent for understanding Holmesian pique was: *It's not fine. You may be a doctor but I am a genius.*

In reply to all of this annoying thinking, John Watson stepped closer to Sherlock Holmes.

Sherlock, being a genius and all, registered the man's proximity at the same time as the warm breath, at the same time that John took his hand—the one with thin scars on the back— legacy of working too fast, of scab-picking boredom, of self-destructiveness.

John looked at the back of the pale hand, then at Sherlock. Then the hand. Then Sherlock. John then said, waving the hand around because clearly anyone with such a hand was absolutely daft, "I mean how do you even cross the street without falling over?"

There are only two other things John Watson could've said that would have surprised Sherlock more: "I love you," and

"I'm pregnant," and he'd get around to the one eventually. So startled was Sherlock that he actually went ahead and thought about giving a proper answer. Then his brain went stealth, took control of his mouth, and Sherlock said something else entirely.

"You proposed marriage this evening. You were rejected."

So.

Soulmate.

John'll look up the word in a couple months, he will, because John's a curious man. When he does, the good doctor will find that the definitions read like so:

A person ideally suited to another.

Someone for whom one feels a natural affinity.

A person who understands you.

By a fountain in the middle of a quiet park on a London spring evening, John didn't yet know the multiple meanings of the word soulmate. Though some part of him must have, for right then John went ahead and did what any soulmate would when faced with extreme provocation—he kept his shit together.

So John didn't say *And what business is that of yours?* or *Well you can fuck right off, Mr. Sherlock Holmes.* Likewise John didn't look at the ground, the trees, or the sky, flushing with the shame of having been rejected. Most importantly and the rarest of all these behaviours, John Watson didn't move right the hell away from a man who shouldn't have known what he knew.

Nope, what John did right then was somewhere down deep recognise who Sherlock Holmes was and then he did what Sherlock Holmes' soulmate would obviously do. He said, "How on earth did you know that?"

Sherlock didn't know what John somehow kind of knew, but he knew John shouldn't have replied quite so kindly, so Sherlock replied kindly.

"You've bought a very nice Savile Row suit from Gieves & Hawkes."

This specificity did not give John a moment's pause. "You guessed I'd proposed to someone by my suit?"

"I deduced it. I'm a freelance detective. The only one."

"That's how you knew I was a doctor? Before?"

"Yes."

Two men came up to the fountain. John glanced at them. Sherlock turned around and walked away.

As John was somehow still clutching Sherlock's scarred hand—but only for another moment—he followed.

John's curiosity kept him quiet, and a raucous group of six walkers coming up behind them kept Sherlock silent, too.

When the group had passed John said, "What else?"

Sherlock sucked in a quick breath, as if he'd forgotten John was there. They started up the rise of Parliament Hill. That was good. Plenty of room.

"Your tie bears the crest of a maker that went out of business a dozen years ago. Your shoes are polished but the style's ten years old. Your wallet—which you switched from a front pocket to the back when you knelt beside the fox—appears twice that. The expense of your suit belies the thrift evident in all of these, so clearly you splurged on a tailored suit to suit a special occasion."

They reached the brightly-lit summit of the hill and Sherlock looked around, as if preparing for flight.

John didn't notice because he felt like his brain was either on fire or made of mush. Or both, which was intriguing and—

"Ouch."

—a bit painful. For the life of him John was having trouble having any other thought than "well *that* was ridiculously sexy" except the other thought he was having which was—

"Why?"

"What?"

Again Sherlock seemed surprised John was still there.

John closed his eyes. This made it much easier for his brain. "I meant how, how did you know I was going to propose."

"I can see the ring-shaped box in your pocket."

John grinned, as if this was the finest observation yet. "Keep going."

Usually Sherlock does. Keep going. Because that's all he's got really, the words that explain what other people don't see. What they sometimes don't see even after he shows them.

"Your jacket and the trousers bear no wrinkles, so you met your companion close by. Once they arrived you didn't get a chance to sit down to dinner or drinks. Again, no wrinkles on your clothes. Well, not until you—"

The word rescue didn't leave Sherlock's mouth but they both heard it anyway.

John stopped under lamplight, glanced up at a dance of moths overhead. He smiled. "Go on."

Sherlock stood just out of arm's reach, as if for safety. "You've been twisting the army insignia ring on your finger, but there's no pale skin beneath it so you don't wear it except on special occasions. Likely a gift from your prospective spouse then, maybe the ring even matched one they had, making them as rare as yourself, a doctor and soldier."

John hummed and the sad thing was that the hum was sad. A grown man trying to let out hurt too big to hold in. "That was why it seemed we could...I just thought... She said no before I even had a chance to ask."

Sherlock Holmes is good at understanding why human beings steal and lie, he's not so good at why they love. Not when love seems to leave behind as much heartache as theft and lies.

"She said no because you're gay."

An awful lot of things began to happen then.

John blurted loudly, "Oh Christ."

Sherlock stepped back. Such words were usually the opening salvo to many other words, none of them kind.

John stepped forward and just then, right then, things switched over into an almost cinematic slow motion and somehow Sherlock had a. very. long. time. to watch Dr. Watson's mouth crook up in a smile, then watch him bow his head to look at his stumbling feet. In reality these took about as long as these things take, but it felt as if Sherlock had all the time in the world to see what he was seeing.

What he was seeing was John Watson's arms rising.

His nails were manicured, short-trimmed and buffed to a moderate sheen, visible even under lamplight. Because the man's hands were not otherwise pampered-looking the good doctor had clearly gone the extra mile this evening as regarded personal grooming.

John Watson had had his suit carefully tailored. As his arms came up, up, up, toward Sherlock's shoulders, Sherlock observed that the cuffs of the doctor's white-starched shirt stuck out precisely one and one half inches from his suit coat. Men unfamiliar with suits, which is to say any man who buys off the rack, will find that the length of a suit coat suits the average man only five percent of the time, such coats being generally cut long so as to appeal to a wider range of men.

Sherlock's long since learned that people are a mess of contradictions and while others might look at this man with the serious eyes and think he lacked vanity, Sherlock was unsurprised to notice John Watson dyed his hair. No, wrong. John Watson tinted his hair, but only at the temples. This close it was possible to see the barest eighth of an inch of grey where follicle met face. This suggested, though did not guarantee, that the woman to whom he'd intended to extend his hand in marriage was perhaps younger than himself.

There was one final thought Sherlock had in that taffy-pulled time of John's fall and that was this: It had been a little bit of forever since anyone had touched him. In those long. long. moments of John Watson's lifting arms reaching for him, Sherlock realised he couldn't remember the last time he had been held.

Sherlock cut off that realisation in favour of the next one: As John Watson lifted his arms Sherlock understood that he was raising his own, *he was reaching back.* He wanted to touch this man who was set to touch him and—

—that's when time snapped like over-extended rubber, right back into place, because John Watson caught his balance, stopped his fall, and smiling said, "Tripped on my own feet."

Fast as a light doused, John's grin washed away because John could see so many things high up on this hill, as bright as if under a spot.

There was St. Paul's off in the distance, the Gherkin too. There was a city spread out below them bright with blue lights and red, big and glowing and far away. What John Watson saw most clearly though was the flush of blood rising fast in Sherlock's cheeks, then the paleness of embarrassment. He saw with the sharpness of peripheral vision two arms falling and then fisted hands ineffectually seeking coat pockets.

"It's lonely being lonely alone," said John. Even to his own ears he sounded like an idiot.

"Yes," sighed Sherlock, as if to a fine deduction indeed.

John nodded, felt like touching Sherlock. Didn't.

"She didn't say no because I'm gay. She never knew. Why would she, it took me years before I did. But you, well you figured it out in twenty minutes."

"Ten."

John grinned. Then apropos of nothing he said, "A freelance detective? I bet I know why your client stood you up tonight."

Sherlock stood so straight so quickly his spine crackled. "How did you know a client stood me up?"

"No idea. Not the point. The thing is, you need to change your name."

Sherlock felt like touching John, mostly in the region of the face, holding him steady so Sherlock could peer into the doctor's eyes and see how he *saw*. Sherlock didn't.

"You see, no one's going to go to a freelance detective. It's like a doctor."

John Watson began to walk toward the city's lights, tugged Sherlock by the cuff as he did so. Sherlock let him.

"Would you trust me if I was a freelance doctor? You would not! You'd go to a consultant though. You should be a *consulting* detective. The only one in the world."

"How did you know I was meeting a client?"

"I really have no idea, do you want a coffee? I need coffee."

John answered for Sherlock. Sherlock let him.

"Of course you do. I know of a great place, they have perfect banoffee pie. I bet you love banoffee pie."

*

The night they met John Watson deduced some very important things about Sherlock Holmes. John later explained *how.*

"When I'm sad, depressed, introspective, lonely, and at a moderate height, I can apparently deduce my soulmate. Easy peasy."

At these moments Sherlock will usually nod as if he believes John, then he'll take hold of John's face, peer into John's eyes or this time into his ears or up his nostrils, and he'll ask a series of scientific-sounding questions, keen to quantify, understand, unearth.

That Sherlock never does find the combination of variables to produce the results of the night they met is neither here nor there. For all their long years Sherlock devotedly pursues the experiment that is John anyway. John happily lets him.

This is, perhaps, as good a definition of soulmates as any other.

(Sherlock does, indeed, love banoffee pie.)

A Series of Sweet Things

The Touchstone Pub, Bankside—1964

John Watson did not pay one little never mind to the man behind the bar, because John Watson does not come into pubs to socialise. He comes into pubs to drink, and while he is drinking he radiates as many prickly *leave me alone* vibes as he can manage, and John Watson can manage a fuck ton of prickly.

So people leave him alone, he leaves them alone, and if it's a rainy Tuesday and the only bodies in the pub are himself and the barkeep, all the better.

Or it was better, it was damn brilliant for awhile, because the bartender was even more spiky than John, who had said thanks after getting his drink and had received a deep frown in reply.

John Watson, after eighteen months of being mostly-unemployed—because no one hires a surgeon with a visible, fucking tremor, and probably incipient alcoholism—yeah, after all that, John can really get behind the whole stink-eye thing.

So just as John's thinking he'll come back to this pub tomorrow, just about the time he's thinking he's found a comfortable place where he can settle in with a whisky and self-pity, well right about that bloody time the damn bartender leans on the bar, bends at the waist and he *moans,* absolutely open-mouthed moans, as if a damned harpoon's just gone through him.

John decides to ignore the man because that's what incipient alcoholics do, but the problem with incipient is it means just beginning, fledgling, only *starting*. There's another part of John that's still bigger than his self-pity and that's his god damn *kindness*. John'll get muddy helping a goose get free of a piece of wire that's trapped it fast, he'll make silly faces at a weeping baby in the park when the father looks like he's about to fall apart, and John'll stand up so fast to get to a hurting human being that he'll knock over his whisky, a double, no ice.

"Where does it hurt," he asks because, though he can see where it hurts—the man's fists are pressed against belly and chest—the asking helps a person focus on something *other* than the hurt.

The bartender groans, stumble-trips away and to his knees, and he looks for all the world as if he's about to crawl under the bar and hide in shadow like a wounded cat.

Which is *exactly* what he's about to do. Crawling to safety is what Sherlock Holmes did last month after he got hit in the head with a pipe and couldn't *see* the killer, it's what he did when he was ten and one kid punched him so badly he couldn't breathe, it's what he will do every single time his brilliant brain and what it helps him see put him in danger and he can't fight back. Because Sherlock doesn't care about pride, Sherlock will hide in the dark and he'll *live* thank you, he'll come back tomorrow or the day after and he'll see what people keep telling him isn't there, he'll *make* them see, even if it means lead pipes or posing as a bartender in a dodgy pub or—

John Watson goes to his knees under that bar, right down there where the fetid water's collected from the broken bar sink, right there where rubbish no one ever sweeps up crusts in the corners, and with steady hands he touches the bartender's forehead, the pulse in his neck. He peels back an eyelid and John can see in those wild skittering eyes that the man wants to push him away, that he reads all the signs of John's help as potential hurt, and when the man half-succeeds, scooting backward with heels scraping against the filthy floor, John gets behind him and sits down hard, so that the man shoves himself backward and into John's open arms.

"It's going to stop hurting," John lies. "I'm going to make it stop hurting, okay, can I do that, will you let me do that?"

The man is hot and cold, sweating but John can feel it prickling his skin with goosebumps. He's still pushing, trying to crawl away from the pain but there's nowhere to go but deeper into John's arms. Wrapping one across the man's chest, scrabbling for the telephone with the other hand, John holds the man fast but the man keeps fidgeting so John keeps dropping the phone and now he's moaning in deep hurt again, so John dips his head, presses his mouth to the man's ear and murmurs low low low, "Hush, love, be still. Shhh."

Immediately the man settles.

For a long moment.

Two.

Three.

Four…and then he fidgets again and John *does* it again, warm lips to an ear hidden beneath a sweat-damp mess of hair, "Hush, it's all right, shhh."

But the man doesn't hush and it's not all right, not until John gets it, flash-quick and clear as day, so he presses his temple against the man's and he whispers close, so his breath is warm right on down the man's neck, "Be still little love, be still."

The man stills.

"There's a sweetheart, thank you."

Finally John gets his call through. He spends most of it barking out facts to medical personnel, then pausing to hum sweet things into a stranger's ear. The operator's replies never stray to *did you just call me angel?* or *are you talking to me?* She's heard every possible thing on the A&E switchboard and before a minute is up, help is dispatched.

John drops the phone, wraps his other arm around the man who has started to moan again and John whispers, "What's your name, sweetheart?"

Sherlock Holmes counts his heartbeats but he can't get past one, so he counts John's words but he can't get past sweetheart, and his chest and belly and head hurt so badly and he's not sure what happens but it feels like there's lips against his other ear and oh, oh, the man has moved and *sweetheart, love, talk to me, come on angel* are filling him up and so he stammers, "Sh-Sherlock."

"What a pretty name. It sounds like a mystery, doesn't it? Mine's John. That sounds…that sounds…hmmm…"

"S-ssssstron—" hisses Sherlock, but he can't finish.

John holds Sherlock tighter and rocks him gently, "Tell me why you're sick sweetie, do you know? Can you tell me?"

Sherlock does tell him, but not until two hours later, in a hospital room, because help arrives then, and things move so very fast.

And then they are clock-tick slow and quiet, John by Sherlock's hospital bed.

They'll release him in a couple hours, but right now he's receiving fluids, weak and alert. John is asking him questions, and Sherlock is answering.

"—once I learned of Mr. Rossetti's symptoms, I suspected his wife. She dusted the pub with powdered kapok, to which a rare few are allergic. The immune response for a healthy but sensitive man would be extreme but not fatal. Chemotherapy had left Mr. Rossetti with an immune system far from strong." Sherlock shrugs. "But I had no proof. The police couldn't search without proof." Sherlock shrugs again.

It doesn't take any kind of genius to understand what Sherlock's not saying, so John says it for him. "So you exposed yourself, because you're allergic to kapok, too."

It's here Sherlock shuts down tight. He doesn't answer because he doesn't want to *be* answered. He doesn't want to hear disbelief, mockery, a "well, that was a stupid thing to do." So Sherlock Holmes says nothing. John is not so reticent.

"You are…a god damn…" Sherlock's already scowling, turning to look out an over-bright window. "…genius."

John steps closer, *peers* at Sherlock. "You knew how much it would hurt and you *let it happen.*"

Sherlock turns. John's smile is—Sherlock can't think of the word for it right now but he will later, he'll think of the word and that word will be *angelic*—wide, admiring, and John says softly, as if right against Sherlock's ear, "It's against every human instinct to let ourselves be hurt, it takes so much bravery to calmly walk into that kind of suffering."

John sits beside the bed and for a moment he reaches for Sherlock's hand and then shyly he doesn't, just rests it on the blanket.

"Will you do me a favour?"

Sherlock's brief joy at the admiration is tempered to resignation. Ah, here it comes. *Go here now, look at this, what about that other case.* After Sherlock does his Sherlock *thing,* he's grown used to thank yous that aren't, thank yous that ignore what he just did by asking him to do more, but that's not what he gets now.

Except he does.

"Just a small favour? Please?"

Sherlock's not holding John's hand, nor John his. Their hands are resting together, side by side on the bed, close enough to feel the warmth from each other's skin. Sherlock looks at those hands and says, "Yes."

The first months back from Aden nearly killed John. When he was still over there he'd sometimes got letters from the soldiers that had gone home, strangely short letters. John had promised himself that when he got home he'd write long letters. He'd write great letters.

But John didn't. John doesn't. Because he learned fast that if he wrote letters to the men he left behind they'd contain nothing but the breathless refrain: *There's nothing to do. There is nothing for me to do here.*

Yet sometimes, if a man is lucky, if a man *looks,* he finds something to do.

"Let me help."

Sherlock blinks. "What?"

"Next time, whatever you're doing, let me help."

Sherlock shakes his head, confused. *"What?"*

"I could have helped reduce the severity of your allergic reaction…I could have helped it not hurt you so badly."

More blinking. Realisation. "Oh."

John smiles that smile again, the one Sherlock will later tell him is angelic, but right now Sherlock doesn't know how to behave around that smile, so he looks out the window again, saying, "Yes."

John looks out the window now, too. "Thank you, love. Thank you."

They both grin as if the bright, bright day is glorious.

Because He's a Lady

Saint Bartholomew's Pathology Museum, London—1889

Cecil Creechurch felt justified in jotting detailed notes of the things Mr. Holmes did in the back of his cab.

Mr. Creechurch felt it proper to sketch Mr. Holmes in his more amusing disguises. He sold both of these to the *Illustrated Police News.*

Finally, the old driver also believed himself justified in overcharging Mr. Holmes slightly, or sometimes taking him to his destination the long way round.

"Evening Mr. Holmes. Where to?"

"Saint Bartholomew's Hospital, Mr. Creechurch."

The horse tossed her head and huffed. Creechurch made soothing sounds. "Been much to-do there lately, sir. Some violence I hear."

"Not to worry," said Sherlock Holmes, tugging up his skirt and crinoline and stepping daintily into the hansom, "I'm certain the Women's Franchise League will do us no great harm."

The cabbie frowned, and joined his horse in huffing.

This, this right here was why Cecil Creechurch, father of two grown children, widower, and cabbie since before Victoria was queen, felt justified in taking with Mr. Holmes certain liberties.

He considered it danger money.

*

Dr. John Watson stood just inside the doors of St. Bart's beautifully odd museum, looking pretty.

Which is to say the good doctor wore a finely-brushed top hat, shining-white collar, a button hole merry with a green carnation, and smiled politely at each guest.

Converged in the airy, high-roofed pathology museum after an extensive talk on universal suffrage, the group of one hundred women conversed over tea and biscuits, roaming amidst thousands of spirit-filled pots, inside which pathological specimens floated.

John's purpose at these quarterly gatherings was always the same: the doctor was there in case someone swooned.

They rarely did. Though the museum's vast collection was a bewitching sort of grim—replete with tumourous growths, infected hearts, and severed body parts, all serenely buoyant in sparkling glass jars—most who came were prepared for what they'd find.

The exceptions had been a lady last year, suffering from a light-headedness John blamed on her blasted corset, while a few years previous a gentleman of self-admitted 'delicate sensibilities' had passed out cold, thumping his head against the spiral staircase. He'd needed three stitches.

Such moments came rarely, so what John mostly did during these evening tête-à-têtes was to eat too many funeral biscuits, answer any medical questions a guest might put to him, and study the visitors for any sign of…anything.

In that very spirit, John took up residence beside the wrought-iron swirl of the staircase, a pile of biscuits on his plate, and John Watson searched for signs.

Sherlock Holmes paid the doctor absolutely no mind.

A black cameo pinned to the lace collar high on his throat, a half-veiled poke bonnet perched on his head, and lace-gloved hands touching, touching, touching, the world's only consulting detective was not in this museum to socialise with the women-only group, he was there pretending to *be* one while searching thousands of jars for proof.

He had suspected finding that proof would be easier than it had been to find ladies' button-up boots in his size or a collar high enough to hide what ladies simply do not have.

Sherlock however, had been wrong, simply not counting on the presence of more than four thousand specimens on multiple-mezzanine levels. It was going to be as difficult to find the one jar he needed as it had been to tighten the laces of his corset.

(Mrs. Hudson had refused to help, mostly because she was unable, giggling so hard she'd gone breathless.)

Speaking of which.

High up on the third level Sherlock pressed a hand to his chest, fruitlessly willing a deep breath down past the corset's constriction. He didn't understand how women wore such a contraption but, then again, that was part of why this group had gathered and…

…Sherlock swayed, clutched at the mezzanine's iron railing until his head cleared. "Come on man!" he hissed to himself, raking his gaze over thousands of glittering jars, searching for the one pot he needed.

Time was of the essence! Tomorrow morning the besotted Earl of Earlham would sign away his lands to a young lady he believed to be his long-lost daughter. The woman was nothing but a fraud and Sherlock nearly had the proof for in one of these pots rested the severed hand of the Earl's true daughter, the limb still faintly bearing the familial birthmark.

"Ah!" said Sherlock, at last spying the jar he needed, right behind the reedy-tall curator, who chatted with a half dozen other women near the skeletons. Hurrying gleeful down the spiral staircase, Sherlock was slowed briefly when his bustle caught on the railing, then slowed rather permanently by an unexpected fit of fainting.

*

Sherlock opened woozy eyes to find a small, wood-walled office around him and beside him a moustachioed man, unbuttoning his blouse.

Sherlock let him.

"—and I don't even know what you were thinking when—"

It was as the grumbling man was undoing Sherlock's third button that the good detective remembered he was a lady. Standing bolt upright, Sherlock clutched demurely at his shirt waist.

Swooning dizzily he sat right back down.

The moustachioed man glowered. "Are you through?"

With one slow hand Sherlock straightened his tipping hat, blinked primly at the man sat beside him, and said absolutely nothing.

John took this as assent, folded his hands on his lap just as fussily as his patient, and said, "Good, that's good. My name is Dr. Watson. John Watson. Now will you unlace your corset or shall I?"

A man not much familiar with women, Sherlock Holmes wrinkled his nose, and tried to think what he was supposed to answer.

Dr. Watson neglected to give him time, instead reaching for Sherlock's gloved hand and plucking it away from Sherlock's bosom. Again the good doctor began to unbutton.

Sherlock let him.

"Tightlacing is simply criminal, it's just, just…it's a terrible thing. It can rearrange your internal organs, you know, damage your bones, and it doesn't let you *breathe* properly, as you found out. As a matter of fact—damn!"

Sherlock complacently sat still for long seconds before remembering he should find such language shocking.

Sherlock opened his mouth to say something, just as quickly closed it. There is the occasional six foot tall woman, lanky and sharp-featured—the museum's curator was just such a one—but it's rare that a woman has a tenore di forza voice.

So instead Sherlock lifted his nose into the air and kept his mouth shut.

"I'm sorry," said the doctor, "But these laces, how did you get them this *tight,* sir?"

Sherlock sniffed in what he hoped was scandalised offense, then said, "Sir?"

Distracted by bone-stiff stays and a fiendish knot, John glowered at Sherlock's corset, then simply took a small knife from his trouser pocket and cut the infernal corset's laces.

Sherlock moaned.

"Are you all right?"

Sherlock slumped boneless on the museum's small office sofa and moaned again. 'All right' did not begin to cover his feelings at this moment. Ecstatic might do. Blissful perhaps. Maybe orgasmic. (As if actually a maiden, this thought caused Sherlock to blush clear up to his eyebrows.)

"I," he said breathlessly, "feel wonderful."

John beamed, patted his patient's lanky leg. "I don't know who helped you into this get-up but I would no longer consider them my friend. The lady should've known those laces were tied much too tight."

Sherlock was too distracted by euphoria to tame his tongue, so he laughed and said, "That lady was me, and I'll take seriously your suspicions. I always did think I was a bit of a bastard."

For long moments Sherlock just smiled at the doctor smiling at him. Then, shoving his bonnet to the back of his head and taking off his lace gloves, Sherlock stuck out his hand. "Sherlock Holmes, consulting detective."

John shook it warmly. "Pleased to meet you Lady Holmes."

Sherlock grinned sly. "You know, one might wonder how you know so very much about women's underthings Dr. Watson."

The doctor nodded politely. "Yes indeed, one might."

"Come now you can speak freely, I'm not *actually* a lady."

The good doctor smoothed his waistcoat and his moustache. "Perhaps not, but *I* am a gentleman."

Sherlock held the other man's eye for twice as long as a man should then, straightening his skirts murmured, "What gave me away in the end?"

Here's the thing: A doctor knows that where one symptom presents, he may unearth others. A *good* doctor gathers these and can then find they lead to a condition, a malady or, in this case, a suspicion.

Tasked with nothing greater than the search for signs of swooning, John had naturally let his gaze wander over the museum crowd. It settled on a tall woman, face half-obscured by a small veil, long fingers flitting from one pot to the next as she roamed restless.

"It was the way you walked in those button-up boots, of course."

Sherlock lifted his chin, for all the world a high-born lady peering at a mannerless mountebank. "I walk flawlessly in these boots."

"And that, sir, is what gave you away. A male's hips are angled differently than that of a female, meaning a man can walk more steadily in heels than a woman. Why just last week I wrapped the ankle of a lady who'd fallen clean off her own heels while strolling along the Strand."

Sherlock sniffed. "Is that all?"

John could have said that once his suspicions were aroused he found other tells. A woman who kept to herself, speaking not once to anyone. A lady too often frustrated by troublesome bustle or loose ribbon. A woman who, when looking at pots overhead, displayed a prominent Adam's apple under taut lace.

Yet, already understanding that before him was a creature both clever *and* vain, John mentioned none of these. "To be honest I didn't really know until you swooned down those steps. When I caught you, you murmured thanks in your natural tenor and then, stumbling, gripped my wrist so tightly it would take a daft man indeed not to suspect."

John rose from the sofa, extended a hand, "Now, what brought Lady Holmes out this evening?"

Pride assuaged, Sherlock primly accepted the offered hand, stood tall and quickly outlined his purpose at the museum, ending with, "—and the tabloids are calling her the Lost Child, sympathetic to the waif. She is, however, neither child nor waif, but a serial fraudster, close to wrongfully inheriting over two hundred thousand pounds that should have belonged to a poor displaced woman whose last remains rest inside this museum."

"The papers are signed first thing tomorrow you say?"

"At dawn."

"It's nearly midnight, we'll need to hurry!"

"We?"

"Of course! You don't think I'd abandon a lady in need do you?"

This, this right here was one of those moments where magic is made or destiny is derailed.

Sherlock Holmes could easily have declined John Watson's unnecessary aid. Yet already understanding that before him was a creature both clever and loyal, instead Sherlock buttoned his blouse, donned his gloves, and rested a lace-clad hand onto the doctor's extended arm.

Four hours later the pot Sherlock had spied before his near-faint was in the hands of the Earl, the fraudulent woman in the hands of Scotland Yard, and Sherlock was again accepting the hand of John Watson, daintily stepping into the back of a hansom cab.

*

For all the little notes Cecil Creechurch made about Mr. Holmes' doings, for all the sketches he drew of the man's amusing get-ups, the old cabbie didn't so much as record the *half* of it.

Though John Watson still occasionally grouses about the Creechurch's penchant for drawing him with a comically large moustache, after moving into Baker Street the good doctor soon learned that the deal struck between the cabman and the consulting detective was an exceptionally fair one.

For the danger to which the old man was sometimes exposed—they still talk about the time the Duke of Claridge tried having Creechurch hanged in retaliation for Holmes' nosiness about gambling debts—the cabbie received his necessary quid-pro-quo.

He sold tall tales and silly sketches to the *Illustrated Police News,* making a nice bit of pocket change, he took the long way round or failed to give change when change was due. And though these things made Holmes and Creechurch quite even, well even so the old cabbie returned a boon to the men of 221B.

Each time the good doctor shared his cab with a mysterious, well-dressed lady, Mr. Creechurch greeted both with a polite nod and complicit grin. He then drove his cab round and round the night-dark edge of Regent's Park, for as many hours as the pair inside wished.

If, through the long evening, there came the laughing of two male voices from inside the hansom, other sounds both dark and deep, or the occasional unsteady rocking of the carriage, why Mr. Creechurch failed to notice these things.

Indeed, for years and years and years, Cecil Creechurch drove around the park, he hummed to his horse, and he noticed absolutely nothing but the pretty London evening.

Deny Thy Nature

Paddington Old Cemetery, London—1924

Cross-legged on a park bench, staring at nothing much, John Watson's gaze flicked back and forth. *Frontal bone, sphenoid bone, ethmoid bone, nasal bone.*

"Fairy."

John hummed tuneless. London's full of chatter and noise. *Zygomatic bone, coronal suture, squamous suture, lambdoid suture.*

"Fairy."

A studying sort of man learns to block noise out. *Parietal bone, occipital bone, temporal bone, maxilla, mandible.*

"Queer."

Especially when he's working hard. *Mandibular condyle, mandibular notch, mandibular ramus.*

"Nancy boy."

John stopped humming. Quietly he put his anatomy textbook on the bench beside him. He uncrossed his legs.

"Poofter."

John stood, turned to the cemetery wall at his back. His skin prickled hot and cold.

"Dirty little shirt lifter."

John was running before he heard the second blow land. Across the park.

Around the wall.

Along the wall to the gate, to the cemetery's gate.

It was chained.

The cemetery's gate was *fucking* chained.

John could hear them, just the other side of the brick wall, angry voices, fists landing, a man moaning.

The gate was chained, it was—

"Police!" John snarled, his voice not his voice at all, deep, furious, the howl of an avenging angel.

"Stay where you are," he roared, rattling the gate to the sudden sound of running feet.

John's gaze flicked back and forth, *one, two*…two pairs of feet fading distant but what about the one they were—another moan high and hurt and John tugged frantic at the gate, saw now that the padlock was open, only hooked through the chain.

He tugged, pulled, ran into the cemetery, fell to his knees beside the curled up man, touched him all over everywhere, searching body and bone.

The man curled tighter so John ran fingers gentle over what he could reach, up into the man's hair, the top and back of his head, his neck…*parietal bone occipital bone, atlas, axis.*

"Fffff," the man stuttered, rolling unsteady to hands and knees, nearly tumbling over the other way. John knee-walked close, danced fingers over the man's face, searching…*zygomatic, mandibular, maxilla*…thought maybe, probably, nothing was broken, nothing too badly hurt.

The man blinked at him, then crawled to a tree and used it to clamber to his feet. John rose right with him. "I'm John," John said, tugging the man's hand away from his own battered eye.

The man pushed a swollen tongue through split lips and slow-slurred, "Shhhhhherlock," then stumbled again, dragging John down with him, their hands scuffing along in the mud and piles of rucked up leaves, and almost immediately Sherlock was trying to leverage himself up again using John's body.

"Stop! You have to stop."

Sherlock did, forehead thunking on John's shoulder. Automatically John cradled the man close, rocked him, shushed soft in the sudden calm. "Yes," he whispered over and over, "Yes, yes, you're fine now." He wondered if this was doctoring, if this was what helping would feel like, warm and right, peaceful and—

"Ffffaggot," Sherlock said, and blink-quick everything changed.

John's brief peace blew away, smoke on the wind. Shame took its place. He let Sherlock go.

Laughing, Sherlock tipped backward onto his rump, and though one eye was swollen shut, blood caked his bottom lip, and mud mucked up nearly into his mouth, he looked at John and laughed and laughed and in case he was really wondering, well there was John's answer bright and clear: No, no, what he'd done wasn't doctoring, it was the opposite in fact. It was selfish. It was wrong. It had been nothing more than sudden desire, dressed up as—

"No," said Sherlock because a rare man can see hands that are now a cold sort of empty, he can see another man trying to hide in plain sight. "No, no, not you."

An even rarer man can see when his words aren't working, but maybe it's only an observant one, a man like a just-turned-eighteen-year-old Sherlock Holmes who knows what will.

"The threats…notes…I know who it was. Tick tick tick." Sherlock tapped at his own forehead then gestured after long-

188

gone men.

Still and barely breathing John said nothing.

Sherlock frowned, grew impatient with his own mutinous mouth. What good was it to see if he could never say what it was he saw?

"It was that word, the American word for..." Sherlock grunted, grabbing the tree again, standing and gesturing artless at everything. "I know who did it, the letters and the threats." He looked down at the man still so very still. No, no, no. It wasn't working, he wasn't getting the words right.

Frustrated, Sherlock pressed palms to eyes and suddenly John was there, right there, pulling at cuffs again. "Stop touching it, where are you going, and why did they call you those terrible names?"

Sherlock moaned but it wasn't with hurt, it was failure. He fails, every day Sherlock fails to act or think or move like other people. He fails to see obvious things, instead seeing the obscure, he fails to explain why one matters and the other doesn't. Sherlock is forever leaving the right words out and saying the wrong, but in the end it's fine because by the time he knows what to say he's talking to empty air and so it doesn't even matter. Except... plucking at his sleeves was a man who hadn't left, a man who was right there in his face and *listening.*

"Not terrible, no, because now I know who sent those letters."

Without thinking Sherlock tried to touch his face again and John stopped him again, and both lost patience, tugging and tripping, but only one said in the voice of a mother fucking avenging angel, "Bloody well stop touching it!"

And Sherlock damn well did.

Another wobble-legged mess of motion, John propped Sherlock against a gravestone and babbled, "Your hands are dirty you'll get it infected, why would you want them to hurt you like this?"

Sherlock fails every day it's true but he doesn't have to always, does he? He looked at the listening man, the one it seemed would. not. leave. him. He opened his mouth to explain why his own bruises were perfect, why his aching eye was wonderful, but when he opened his mouth nothing came.

Yet here's the thing: John Watson wasn't studying medicine because he thought he'd be a great doctor, or had a driving need to be a surgeon. No, the thing with John was he knew when someone hurt. A headache, a heartache, it didn't matter, John always knew.

He didn't always know what to do about it, but that was what textbooks were for, the repetition, the late nights. In the meantime he did the best healing he could by guessing.

"Are you ashamed? Of being—"

"No," Sherlock keened, frustrated at words bunched up, at thoughts in his head that never, ever made it to his mouth.

Pushing off the gravestone, scuffing toward the general direction of the city, John was beside him again and that felt right, to Sherlock that felt right and suddenly they were there, a muddy rush of words. "My tutor, Dr. Caitiff, the threats in the notes, all those names, they called him all of those same names. They said he'd be hurt if he talked. He'd be hurt until he *couldn't* talk. I know who sent the notes."

"One of the men who did this?"

Sherlock grinned so big his lip bled fresh. He let John hold him up on his rubbery-lead legs and Sherlock giggled giddy and whispered right against John's ear, "It was a man. But not the one I thought."

In the last two hours a headache had taken root behind Sherlock's eyes, his body had bloomed with new bruises, but oh, the thing that had flowered most vigorous was Sherlock's anger.

Sat on his hospital bed like a straight-backed king, he glared at the walls and thought dark thoughts of traitorous John Watson.

Solid arm slung round Sherlock's waist in that muddy graveyard, steady steps taking them together *out* of it, John had been deceptively deferential, distracting.

"So who did what and why?" He'd asked, going and doing that miracle of listening again, and maybe Sherlock was already familiar with the cant of the man's head, the steadiness of his watchful eye, because for the first time a cascade of the right words came and Sherlock poured them out and right into John Watson's ear.

"Dr. Caitiff was my first year chemistry tutor. An entirely conventional man in experimental outlook, he's bored and boring, moving in dissatisfaction toward a retirement he neither wants nor can avoid as his arthritis leaves him more infirm.

"I'd forgotten him entirely until he approached me a few weeks ago, bringing five letters he'd received over the last several months. The letters were crude things, written in a crude hand, full of vicious threats and epithet-riddled accusations of homosexuality. Something Caitiff denied to me, using language worse than in the letters."

"So this is a mystery then?"

Walking slowly but nearly unsupported, Sherlock grinned, "It's a puzzle, John, coarse and rudimentary, but a puzzle none the less! A good puzzle's worth a few bruises, yes?"

No, John thought, gaze dancing over a blood-mired chin, at a hand that gripped his arm knuckle-white. *Not like this, no. Not like this ever again.*

"Caitiff heard I'd discovered the source of blackmail letters being sent to a fellow student. He wondered if I could find proof that one of his ex-students was sending these foul letters to him. He said he feared for the sanctity of his life and truly, right then I should have realised something was wrong, but I've a bad habit of presuming a client is my ally."

Sherlock stumbled then, as if awkward over the self-importance of the word 'client.' John shushed gently, which Sherlock took as a sign to speak faster.

"The letters were a confounding mix of erudite and raw—*and I will lay waste to everything you hold dear* coming right after *gonna hurt you yeah*—and Caitiff was sure they were written by a student he'd taught several years ago, Arthur Warrington, 'or by his horrible little friend,' Joseph Galena."

Turning onto windy Edgeware Road, Sherlock again tried to pester his eye but was again obedient to John's grumblings. "Caitiff begged me to find proof, telling me there'd been a threat just that morning scrawled on his office door."

They crossed the busy road quickly, then walked again more slowly, in and out of pools of lamplight.

"I'm no good at human beings, John. I believe liars and find suspicion in truth. I should have talked to more people. I should have made Caitiff prove the provenance of those letters, insist he show me that office door. If I had, I wouldn't have done what I did."

And what Sherlock did was fall in love with the drama of the chase, with the derring-do of detection. He believed his client, and he followed suspects, and he daydreamed triumphant outcomes. Oh he saw and observed what didn't fit—those oddly-phrased letters—but Sherlock Holmes was still learning how to apply science to emotion, evidence to suspicion.

"He told me the door didn't matter, that he was frightened, and I let his panic infect me. I followed Warrington and Galena like he asked and the thing is, they knew who I was, in that graveyard they knew who I was because he'd told them."

"Why?"

"I don't know. I don't know what he thought it would accomplish except for what it did: They made me the scapegoat of their fear and their anger. For Arthur maybe even his own shame. They attacked me instead of him, but in the end that gave me what I needed, it helped me realise who was sending those letters."

John paused at a brightly-lighted corner, as if to catch his breath.

"They vented their fury," Sherlock said, breathless. "You heard them. They called me terrible names, they laid hands on me, the both of them, and somewhere in that madness Joseph struck my mouth. I grabbed his shirt on reflex as I fell and he fell with me, landed on top of me. Three things happened then. I felt the press of breasts against my chest. In my fist I felt the cloth binding them. And I saw what I'd seen but not observed: Joseph's face was smooth."

They walked on again, this time in silence. John let that silence lie, though in future the good doctor would have far less patience with Sherlock's love of dramatic quietude.

Finally, as they stepped through large wood doors and into a small, warm room, John said, "Well? What does it all mean?"

Sherlock grinned wide, one bright eye twinkling, and he pronounced with solemnity and certainty, "Dr. Caitiff sent those letters to himself."

It was then and for the first time since the graveyard that Sherlock observed his surroundings. "We're not at the university."

"Of course not," said John, "we're at St. Mary's hospital. You're being admitted."

*

Sherlock's complaints had fallen on deaf ears, with which St. Mary's staff seemed replete.

While tonight Sherlock had learned a painful lesson in client allegiance, John had no such problem, in minutes locating a doctor who sided with him completely, ignoring Sherlock's refrain of "I'm fine."

That had been three hours ago. Three hours of injections, of frowning at four walls, of rehearsing a sharp-tongued critique of John Watson and his traitorous manners. Woozy hours of trying to remember the things John had said before he left, of…of…three……of……

"It's done."

Opening his eyes to a moon-bright hospital room,

Sherlock's first thought was *damn it, I fell asleep.* His second thought was, "You came back."

Sitting up, a palm pressed to the fluttering weightlessness in his chest, Sherlock grinned giddy again, forgetting every word of his diatribe.

"Course I did."

The ward had long since gone hushed and dark, but in the moon's bright light Sherlock could see John clear enough. "You went to see Caitiff."

"I told you that if you stayed, I would go."

Ah, yes that, that'd been one of the things Sherlock couldn't remember: A promise made for one extracted.

Sherlock lifted a hand and, as if it were quite normal, John placed in it one of his own. Sherlock studied that hand, then pronounced, "No marks. You didn't touch him."

"I told you I wouldn't."

Those had been more of John's words. After the doctor had gone away and the hospital went quiet, they'd talked low and Sherlock had finally explained everything.

"I suppose knowledge must begin somewhere and perhaps I'll be quicker off the mark next time, but Caitiff gave me all I needed those few times we talked. He let slip just enough, making ill-tempered pronouncements about obedience and gratitude, about what boys owe to the men who teach them. I'd made a point to ignore the old rumours, the whispers about what Caitiff did and with whom. His family has long contributed large financial sums to the university, the gossip seemed petty and jealous, colleagues fostering rumours because they wanted to believe Caitiff's tenure had been bought.

"I told you I talked to other people. I don't think Caitiff knew that. Interesting what strangers will tell you if you ask softly, as if you care. Just bits and pieces mind you, because that's all most know, but that's what a puzzle is, John, bits and pieces one must painstakingly put together.

"I didn't figure it out then but it's clear now that there had been an affair between Caitiff and Arthur. Clearly it ended after Arthur graduated, but it seems Caitiff wanted Arthur back. Even more so once he learned about Joseph.

"I understand now why Caitiff told Arthur about me. Because the threats in those letters would mean nothing unless backed by some sort of action. So he told Arthur I was gathering proof that Arthur and Joseph were lovers."

"If you can't have what you want, destroy it."

"Caitiff thinks he has leverage. That if Arthur doesn't come back to him he can expose a love affair between two men. He doesn't know that biologically Joseph is not a man."

"I don't understand all of this," John said, "but that most of all."

"I'm an unsociable sort and don't pay much attention to fellow students, but even I've heard of Joseph Galena. Double-firsts in physics and engineering, he's not yet graduated and already Cambridge, Oxford, and the École d'ingénieurs de l'Université de Lausanne have offered him a place. Though some universities talk a good game, little has really changed, for I imagine none of those venerable institutions would have extended their offer if they knew Joseph Galena is a woman."

John raised a hand for silence. Sherlock complied. "Let me see if I understand." Ticking things off on his fingers, John said, "So Caitiff abuses his power over a student. That student,

Arthur Warrington, leaves him for another once that power becomes moot. Caitiff tries to get him back and when that doesn't work he falsifies abusive letters, says they're from Arthur, and threatens to expose Arthur's supposed homosexual relationship with Joseph."

John raised a questioning brow; Sherlock nodded. "All right. Caitiff then rashly asks your help in finding evidence to prove Arthur means to hurt him, but then he tells Arthur what you're doing. Unaware of Caitiff's duplicity you follow Arthur and Joseph into the graveyard. In a rage they turn on you and do—"

John hands fisted, his expression thunderous. "—terrible things, playing into Caitiff's hands. Now he has proof they're as violent as the fake letters make them sound. But all they were trying to do, however awfully, was protect each other from Caitiff, who never thought you'd figure out that he wrote the letters."

Another raised brow, another nod. "Right then, there's just one thing I don't understand: How did you figure out Caitiff wrote those letters?"

There's nothing that's always been, everything must begin. Sherlock Holmes began his journey toward a certain sort of genius years before this night. Yet his travel had been fitful, rife with wrong turns and scatter-shot effort. Maybe he'd have abandoned the science of deduction if there'd been yet another restless night where puzzle pieces refused to fit, where the silence again went unbroken by any voice but his own.

But that didn't happen. Instead Sherlock Holmes met John Watson and the journey began all over again. Only this time the travelers were two.

"Caitiff made a mistake in those forged letters. You see he'd lived in America before the war and there faggot means something far different than it does here. Neither Arthur or Joseph used the epithet, even at the height of their fury. In the letters Caitiff had used it twice."

There's nothing that's always been, everything must begin. John Watson began his journey toward a certain roguish respectability years before this night. His travel had been straight and true, but in the silence of a few restless evenings he admitted that his journey was also rather...dull.

Then John Watson met Sherlock Holmes and though the path he would follow remained in some ways firmly fixed—John would become a doctor, then a soldier—well that path suddenly contained forks, and the first one John ventured down happened that night.

That was when John rose up and said, "This has to end."

Sherlock had swung his legs over the side of his hospital bed, "Yes."

"No Sherlock, you're not coming."

"What? Then you're not going."

"Sherlock Holmes, I will go directly to your doctor if you take one step away from that bed, I will then walk straight out that door and never return because I do not accept backtalk from a patient."

"You can't have this adventure without—"

"It's not an adventure. It's a life. Lives. Including yours. I'll talk to Caitiff, that's all. If you stay I'll return and tell you everything. Will you? Will you please?"

Somewhere a clock softly chimed ten o'clock. The sound seemed to linger long after the chime had struck. Somewhere much, much closer a man grumbled, then swore, then swung his legs back into his bed. That man crossed his arms and looked out a moonlit window and pretended he didn't hear a man's quiet departure.

Sherlock hadn't intended on falling asleep but when he woke it wasn't with a scowl or a curse, it was with gratitude.

"You came back," he said.

"Course I did," John replied.

John sat on Sherlock's bed and whisper-chattered what had indeed been something of an adventure.

"I went to the university and he was there. It was quiet and mostly dark and just the two of us. I watched him from the hall, he was scrawling something across the outside of his office door."

"Ah, he finally realised he needed that proof."

"I think he was writing something melodramatic, like 'I will make you pay.' I confess I forget because when I said 'Hello Dr. Caitiff,' he startled so badly he threw the chalk at me."

John rubbed at his bloodshot eye. Pinching John's sleeve in two fingers Sherlock tugged and scolded. "Stop touching it."

They both laughed and as quickly sobered.

"What happened after?"

"I told him to step into his office."

"Told."

"Yes."

"And what did you say to him there?"

"Mostly I named all the bones in his body."

"There are more than two hundred."

"Yes."

Sherlock bit his lip.

"Then I told him which bones don't heal very well after they break."

Sherlock made a noise.

"Then I told him some truths and maybe a few lies."

Sherlock's tongue slicked over his lips, as if tasting something sweet.

"I told him everything you'd deduced. Then told him I'm a doctor, that Arthur Warrington and Joseph Galena are my friends. I told him that you and I would help should either of them ever need to...hide something."

Sherlock was now breathing through his mouth.

Somewhere deep in the half-empty hospital a clock chimed midnight. Sherlock counted out loud. "One, two, three, four," and John knew he was tallying the hours since they'd met. It was just a few, only a few. Barely a lifetime.

Strange though, how much life a man can live in so little time. How certain things take you both by *hello,* on past *nice to see you again,* far beyond *you intrigue me,* and right up hot-breath close to something certain and true.

You.

I choose you.

Through their long life together most will call John Watson Sherlock Holmes' friend. They'll call him his biographer, his doctor, his partner.

From this day forward what John would really be was Sherlock's avenging angel. His one true love.

And Sherlock would be John's.

Uncivilised

Near Montague Street, London—1987

"The garrotter turned out to be a primary school teacher!"

"That's not my fault!"

"You suggested I take the case!"

"Liar!"

"Mr. Holmes."

"If you find the truth difficult to hear Detective Sims, I assure you that's not *my* fault!"

"Mr. Holmes."

"And, if you'll remember, *detective,* I told you the man didn't have the mental acuity to plan one, much less three grisly—"

"Mr. Holmes!"

Sherlock Holmes, Detective Sophia Sims, and possibly the museum curators walking down Montague Street, abruptly stopped talking.

Mrs. Zabriski cleared her throat, looked at her ever-irksome tenant, his Scotland Yard visitor, then passed a meat cleaver from her right hand to her left. "Thank you. Now, I paused in my dinner preparations and came up three tiresome flights of stairs to ask you to speak like civilised human beings in my home."

Sherlock opened his mouth to argue the absurdness of this absurdity but Mrs. Zabriski, three times Sherlock's age, nearly half his weight, yet two times tougher than he would ever be *ever,* scratched delicately at her temple. With the back of the meat cleaver.

Sherlock Holmes shut his mouth.

"I'm usually willing to let you cry it out boy—"

Sherlock opened his mouth. With a fast flash of the meat cleaver Mrs. Zabriski cut a loose thread from the hem of her Sunday-best blouse. Sherlock closed his mouth.

"—so to speak, because I know how frustrating you find it when these little cases of yours seem promising, when the kleptomaniac clown turns out to have been in Brighton or buggering about with a stripper, but I've a dozen things to do—including take special delivery of a new rug to replace the old rug you so helpfully burned—and I'm afraid listening to you and Miss Detective Sims shout is trodding on my last nerve. Now I've one question: Are there any questions?"

Right about then Zabriski's meat cleaver caught a bit of afternoon sun with a merry little shimmer.

No one said a word.

"Good," said Sherlock's landlady, "Now Mr. Holmes, I am presuming you have time to nip down to the pub and fetch me a bit of rum for my rum cake, yes? Mr. Fleure owes me…" Mrs. Zabriski smiled in a manner quite uncivilised. "…we'll just say the man owes me. A pint bottle will more than do."

As Sims let herself out, Mrs. Zabriski followed but paused in the doorway of her tenant's chaotic studio flat and said darkly, "And Sherlock, if you annoy Mr. Fleure I will…"

The meat cleaver caught the bright winter light.

*

To show his landlady that she was absolutely not the boss of him, Sherlock Holmes did not immediately go to the pub round the corner to fetch her rum.

Instead he walked across the road to see if the dry cleaner had successfully removed from his best suit the camel dung flung at him by the homicidal zookeeper (he had). He strolled to Euston station to get two pasties from old Mrs. Grace (she pinched his cheek). Then Sherlock went to Regent's Park to feed bits of one pasty to his favourite duck (she quacked).

Eventually the consulting detective strolled into the Nail & Hammer pub as if he were a regular. In truth, he'd never once been. And never would again, though he did not yet know this.

What Sherlock did know was that, as he placed his hands on the bar, a hand was placed upon his arse.

Sherlock looked at the bar. It was but the matter of a moment to deduce that, as the two hands in front of him were his own, the one on his arse was not. Sherlock looked at the big man beside him and said—

"Hello gorgeous."

—absolutely nothing. Because Sherlock recognised the big man with the roaming hand as the pub owner's son. The good detective knew this because old Mrs. Grace had once pointed him out. "Oh, that's Mr. Fleure's son, Bern. Used to be such a good boy. Creepy as fuck, now."

The sixteen stone Bern grinned down at Sherlock and said, with a lot of damp lip-licking, "Such a good-looking man."

Flick-flick-flick, Sherlock's gaze razed over the junior Fleure.

Nearly-blind in one eye. Drug addict. Divorced. Broke.

And hiding them all.

Bern stepped close, breathed beer fumes right in Sherlock's face. Sherlock grinned feral, ready to say things, oh so many *delightful* things.

He got as far as opening his mouth, ready to delight himself in the saying of these things, but instead Sherlock Holmes *remembered* things.

Mrs. Zabriski's face when he'd accidentally burned her rug to ash.

Mrs. Zabriski's face when his sulfur experiment forced the clearing of half a dozen flats.

. *Mrs. Zabriski's meat cleaver catching the light.*

And Sherlock remembered what happened the last time he'd done what he wanted instead of the simple thing he was asked.

No, he did not want to move again. Not again. It was…it was fine. Just *fine*. Sherlock would behave like a civilised person, he did know how. He'd keep his mouth shut, he'd get the ridiculous rum, and then, since the latest Scotland Yard 'detective' had showed up and ruined another case, he'd just spend the evening culturing his *moulds*.

Sherlock dropped the wild from his mouth but not his eyes, stared hard into Bern's good eye until he saw he was seen, then…then…a placid-looking man behind Fleure was staring hard at Sherlock.

Soldier. Doctor. Bored. And…

Sherlock followed the placid man's grinning gaze to Bern's mostly-full pint. Salt grains, just a few, were scattered like tiny stars on the bar top.

…and uncivilised.

"Sorry, sweetheart." The man said, stepping around Bern as if the giant were not there. He kissed Sherlock's cheek. "I know I'm late but we really have to go or we'll *both* be late."

The placid man's eyes stared into Sherlock's. *Go, go, we have to go now.*

Sherlock let the wild back in with a grin and, staring at Bern, he put his hand on the back of the placid man's neck, kissed his temple with all the familiarity of a lover. "I was just waiting for you my dear."

Bern frowned a few long seconds, slicked a wet tongue over his lips, and then Bern Fleure did what John Watson and Sherlock Holmes both knew angry drunks do: He grabbed his pint and drank the entire thing down in one breath.

Bern was lucky. The vomiting only *really* kicked in once he was inside the gents.

*

John and Sherlock were several streets away by then, draped dramatically breathless over a park bench and giggling like school boys.

"Terrible," keened one.

"Ridiculous," howled the other.

"Awful."

"Absurd."

"Brilliant."

"Oh yes, very much that." Wheezing, Sherlock flailed a long arm to his right. "Sherlock Holmes."

Sloppily taking the hand offered, the no-longer-placid man laughed and huffed, "John Watson, but call me John 'cause I think we're engaged now."

Here's the thing: John Watson and Sherlock Holmes did not shake one another's hand for a single second longer than two strangers do. They did not at that moment sense in one another a kindred spirit. They certainly didn't feel a fine frisson of attraction skittering down spines and sparking hot in groins.

No, none of that happened just then. However, years from now, when they talk of this moment on quiet nights in a warm bed? Oh, then they very much do remember those few breathless moments exactly that way, they remember them as the beginning of everything.

Right now though, Sherlock breathed deep and slumped onto the bench beside John, said in high admiration, "You salted his beer."

Hands on knees John splashed a giggle down at his shoes, then looked at Sherlock and, again, it must be said, there was no particular resonating moment of attraction, he didn't gaze into sharp eyes and think *they see me.* No, that revelation wouldn't come for a few hours yet, at a coffee shop tucked away in Angel, but John? John will somehow remember it as happening here, right here on a paint-thick bench, looking into those keen, fine eyes and admitting sotto voce, "Learned that back in med school. Always wanted to see if it worked. Used to be a remedy in Victorian days when they thought purging cured everything."

"Doesn't it?"

It wasn't even funny.

That'll be what John grouses sometime next year, pinching Sherlock's bare arse as if in some sort of delayed bad-joke recompense. Sherlock will agree and then burrow beneath the duvet after his morning prize, laughing then like they laughed in the park right now.

Sherlock thunked his head against the back of the bench and grinned. "It was ingenious."

"Incapacitating a big arsehole with a tiny salt shaker does have a certain elegance," agreed John.

With another skittering of laughter and by silent agreement John Watson and Sherlock Holmes both heaved themselves upright and began walking side-by-side.

"How else could you do it?"

Feeling the best he'd felt in months John a little bit bounced on his toes. "Pardon?"

"Incapacitate a man. How else?"

At the sudden silence Sherlock belatedly remembered: *Ah yes, doctor. A caring profession.*

Then, to prove he wasn't a really big arsehole but instead a man of learning, Sherlock Holmes said, "A head butt to the nose is only effective for like-sized individuals, a knee to the groin usually leads to weepy moaning which draws too much attention, and the one time I boxed someone's ears their spike earring cut open my palm."

John Watson stopped bouncing on his toes. He stopped walking. Yet, instead of hastily remembering a previous engagement, the good Dr. Watson leaned close to the curious Mr. Holmes and murmured, "What the hell *are* you?"

As if offering a state secret Sherlock leaned back and whispered, "Consulting detective."

And, as if *this* was completely self-explanatory, John began bounce-walking again and said, "Oh. Well. A solid kick to the shins hurts like hell and effectively hobbles your attacker." John glanced at Sherlock's feet. "Yeah, a pair of Fratelli Borgiolis would do the trick."

Half a year from now, completely in love, totally drunk, and celebrating their six-month anniversary on the roof of 221B, Sherlock will lean conspiratorially close to John and murmur, "That's when I knew. You're the only ex-army doctor I've ever met who recognised Borgiolis at a glance."

Half a year from now, clutching an empty wine bottle, totally in love, and with his head in Sherlock's lap, John will nuzzle and say serenely, "I'm the *only* ex-army doctor you've ever met."

That would be then. Right now Sherlock smiled at the fancy-shoe-recognising doctor, and as they rounded a corner he opened his mouth to say something urbane and witty but instead he grunted, stopping abruptly. Both men stared at the pavement in front of them.

A heap of clothes, shoes, and shattered lab equipment rested at their feet.

John looked from the clothing, to Sherlock. Sherlock looked from John to most of his worldly possessions.

"My landlady may have found my hidden mould experiment. And I her last nerve."

Sherlock drifted forward. Toed at the broken Petri dishes. Most were covered in furry mould mounds of brown and blue. There were a few festive reds and greens.

John came close, gestured. "That's a gorgeous penicillin. The other one Hemitrichia serpula?"

Sherlock surreptitiously kicked a shrunken human head under a splay-paged copy of *Advanced Analytical Toxicology*. "Thank you. Yes."

"Hmmm," John said, watching the head rolling gently away.

Sherlock hmmmed in reply and they both scratched the backs of their necks.

This would have been a good time to shake hands, part ways, and go on with their lives. They both had that choice, oh yes they did.

And here's the thing: Both knew these next few seconds could change everything, that life need not go on as it always had done but that the change depended, oh so very much, on what they would do next.

So.

Despite the shrunken human head—or maybe because of it—John Watson squatted down in front of Sherlock's possessions, tugged out a jackknife sunk deep into a dart board, said, "A friend of mine. She's got a place to let on Baker Street. Interested?"

The good doctor stepped back, flicked his wrist. The jackknife quivered in the dart board's bull's eye. "If you don't mind an invalided ex-army doctor as a flatmate."

Sherlock Holmes blinked a couple dozen times at the knife, his stout heart doing a merry skittery-thump. He looked up at John. He grinned. "How could I say no to my fiancé?"

John Watson grinned back. It was positively *uncivilised.*

Inevitable

Quite a Number of Places In London—2008, 2009, 2011, 2012, 2013

"I will give you a week of my holiday leave John. I'll give you that scarf of mine you like so much. I'll buy you a hot chocolate. John? *John?"*

Dr. Magdalena Abejas waved a hand in front of her young colleague's face. After the third pass he blinked.

"Sorry," he said, "I was just wondering if you knew you went in entirely the wrong direction with those. Then I realised we don't really have time to discuss it. Why are you still here? Go, *go!"*

Dr. Abejas made a high sound, somewhere between panic and glee. "I only need five minutes. I've told Mr. Holmes you'll be with him while I'm gone. I'll just nip right up there and right back. She says it's nothing, but I'm a doctor and I know nothing is never not something."

Instead of wondering if Magdalena knew that she was also a hypochondriac along with being a physician, John made shooing gestures. "I'll stay with Mr. Holmes. Go, it's fine."

Before John had finished, the expectant mother, chronic worrier, and senior physician in the small surgery in which John Watson worked, was pounding up two flights of steps to the obstetrics clinic headed by her pregnant girlfriend.

With a deep breath, a smile, and a sudden craving for hot chocolate, John turned, tapped on the consulting room door and said, "Mr. Holmes?"

By the criterion used by people who are not doctors, John Watson is a good doctor. Which is to say beyond his diagnostic abilities or his score on Healthgrades, John is kind and he is polite.

So as he quietly closed the consult room door behind him, clasped his hands…and fast-blinked at Mr. Holmes' bare arse.

Magdalena had failed to mention the thing for which she was treating her patient. John now felt she had been remiss in this. For before him was a white man, belly down and face pillowed in crossed arms, wearing nothing below the waist but a bright red bottom.

John tip-toed forward, blinked a half-dozen times at Mr. Holmes' behind, then scooped up Magdalena's notes.

…for what he calls an 'investigative case' got into the aquarium tank with a Lion's Mane jellyfish…

John peered at the thin red lines criss-crossing Mr. Holmes' back end. So inflamed was the area John imagined he could feel the heat of it.

"Mr. Holmes," he said creeping closer, whispering as if the weight of his breath could cause the patient further distress, "I'm Dr. Watson. If there's anything you need while Dr. Abejas is gone please don't hesitate."

Mr. Holmes took a deep breath and…snored.

John cocked an ear. Helpfully Holmes snuffled louder.

John looked at the chart: *Lidocaine.* Ah, excellent. A painkiller. The relief must have been intense, no wonder the man was out cold.

Hours later, John was not. After Magdalena had returned—"False alarm! I knew it would be"—John went home.

Instead of thinking about his pending deployment to Afghanistan, he lay in bed wondering exactly how a man got a stinging jellyfish attached to his hind quarters.

While he reflected on Mr. Holmes' arse, it did not occur to John that he'd never seen Mr. Holmes' face.

*

Not quite a year later Sherlock Holmes adjusted the wicker basket draped over his arm and checked his watch. He could spare no more than five minutes. These body parts would not stay fresh forever.

Standing in an impromptu Scotland Yard interrogation room, with a cluster of detective constables and a DI, he watched live CCTV footage on a wall-mounted screen.

The camera showed fifteen men in a plain conference room somewhere in the bowels of this over-large London gym. On screen some men stood together, some didn't, all expressed various levels of discomfort, impatience, or fear.

Sherlock looked at each man for a few seconds.

"It's the sniveling one on the bench."

The DI scowled. "Sniveling's rather much."

Sherlock nodded brightly. "Yes, exactly!"

"What?"

"Sniveling. It's over-done isn't it? I was a rather weepy child and I remember doing a lot of sniveling. It's a portmanteau of sniffling and crying and most of us stop about the age of six. That white man on the chair at the left? Not only is he sniveling, he's trembling, mumbling, darting his eyes around as if afraid of the shadows. That's too much detail, too lavishly laid on.

Someone that frightened fights to hide it, just as a drunk man struggles to look sober. It's human nature. Instead of being afraid of a potential bomb, he's the one who made the threat."

The detective inspector exhibited her own bit of human nature just then. Crossing her arms, standing tall, she looked down her nose at the consulting stranger. "Yeah, well the cocky bloke in the towel? He's sitting peaceable as you please. Swings right the other way then, doesn't he? Too little detail. As if he's not afraid. As if he knows the threat's an empty one. I say *he's* the one acting suspicious."

That interrogation room was just full of humans exhibiting their nature right then for Sherlock Holmes regally adjusted his hand basket and—here as a courtesy to his brother and uninterested in which of these half-dressed males had texted his threat of a bomb beneath an empty bus—said, "Suit yourself detective inspector, but you'll find that that man—"

Sherlock Holmes and DI Barbeito looked at *that man.*

"—with his military carriage, regulation haircut, and a certain air of both command and compliance, is likely a soldier. Probably on active duty judging from the freshness of the cut— you can see the pale skin left bare on the back of his neck where he had it shaved shorter than he usually wears it. Earlier in the footage he's holding that black man's wrist, working the range of motion, asking questions. Possibly a medic, nurse, or doctor in the field. This would make him both habituated to high-stress situations and able to remain calm in them. His behaviour is the precise opposite of suspicious."

Sherlock glanced into his basket and Barbeito told herself that she did not see within its wicker confines severed human hands.

"I'm having something of a busy night and really must get back to it. Arrest whomever you like. Good evening."

*

The third time John and Sherlock met without meeting they were on the 139 bus to Waterloo Station and John had an erection.

It was not his fault.

He'd been home from Afghanistan not quite a half year now and still hadn't found anyone willing to take him on for more than occasional work. Usually told he was overqualified, people then often asked him the unanswerable, "After the excitement of the army would a man like yourself really be happy in a boring old surgery like ours? I'm afraid all we could offer are lots of silly old sore throats and some flu jabs."

The marvel was that these overweening words had not yet caused John to stand up, lean across the desk of the fuckwaffle uttering them, and hiss in their pontificating face. "I died in Afghanistan. A whole eight seconds they say. Shot in the shoulder so I'll never do surgery again, noted.

"But I'll take the grace of giving flu jabs, I'll happily wipe noses and poke at prostates and whatever else you've got on, because here's the thing, here's the thing you don't get about dying dead and coming back: It makes you grateful.

"So, if you'd kindly stop pretending you're being *kind* and own up to not wanting a possibly-PTSDed ex-soldier in your fancy little Harley Street surgery that'd be lovely. Because you know what? Do you know what? I've got more than gratitude, I've got a shite detector like you would not believe and you are pegging it up past the red."

Right, well John hadn't said those words, not once, not yet.

What John did do was keep going on job interviews. He'd just finished up another one and then wearily got himself onto a rush-hour bus. As the journey was long, he started reading the Gothic vampire novel his flatmate lent him. He discovered too late that it was one of those books of the highly-sexed variety and now he had a boner.

He stopped reading.

About the time John Watson started worrying the crush of bodies would cause him to rub his hard-on against the leg of the man in front of him, the man in front of him, started to yell.

Sherlock Holmes wasn't shouting about a stranger's stiffy however, he was pushing through the bus crowd, pressing every stop-button on the way, shouting "—Aldwych arsonist! Can't you see? Crossing the street! Right there! There! Stop stop stop the bus!"—before clamouring through open doors and off into the night.

*

The fourth time John and Sherlock nearly met was at a St. Mary's Easter party and John was reaching for another creme egg, when a tall man took his outstretched hand, wrapped an arm around his waist, and started dancing John around the room.

"Well that was rude."

"Thank you."

"If that's what you consider a compliment mate, I don't even want to know what you think is an insult."

"Smile, you look all pinch-faced."

"Yeah, that'll do."

"No I mean smile, look like you're enjoying yourself or it'll seem suspicious."

John should have, could have, and maybe in a moment would have asked what suspicion had to do with it, but instead he watched his partner's swift-moving feet, focused on the next few steps of the waltz, and was about to request introductions when his partner let him go.

"Thank you," said the man, then dashed off after a woman carrying an overlarge purse that did not match her finery even a little bit.

*

The fifth time they met it was for good, because even Fate at last understood their inevitability.

So, on a chilly April night, in a gents' toilet, John Watson met Sherlock Holmes.

And most of the rest became history.

*

Sherlock thinks where Sherlock will.

To perform the delicate brain work required to correctly conclude the whereabouts of a disappeared heiress, Sherlock once paused in the middle of Oxford Street on a Friday evening during a bank holiday weekend. He experienced more physical contact in those five minutes than in the previous five months.

While pondering the problem of a missing bit of Chinese pottery, Sherlock recently stopped dead in an open lift door, never noticing the profanities uttered as people pushed past, and only later realising someone had pinched his umbrella.

In an effort to visualise how a man might crack a safe when the only entrance to the room was smaller than his head, Sherlock currently stood at the sink in an over-bright cafe gents, warm water splashing unheeded over his hands.

A minute later Sherlock was still standing at that sink, a kind of Schrödinger's detective—there and not there. In his mouth he could still taste but did not taste blood. He could smell but did not smell the bleach used on the toilet floor that morning. He heard and didn't hear the loo door open and close. And Sherlock Holmes saw and didn't see a man pass by him slowly, silently.

Everything was happening but not happening to *him.* Sherlock stood still in the middle of it, senses shut down but brain open as a box, a box through which he searched with slow and meticulous care for the one clue that offered an answer instead of the thousands that did not.

Behind Sherlock, John Watson was his own sort of slow and meticulous, because a stranger doesn't just approach a stranger.

No, first he comes into a cafe for a coffee, then, about to leave he sees a pair of things. Blood. And blood.

Two drops.

One left of the till, the second beneath the sign pointing to the men's toilets.

That's when John forgot to go back to work and instead did what he'll always do: Follow the blood.

In the loo John found no more gore on the floor, just a man at the far sink washing his hands. John wanted to say something, but a stranger doesn't just approach a stranger, so John went to piss though there was no need.

Afterward he slow-washed his hands and looked into the sink next to his.

A bright circle of blood on the porcelain, a couple inches up from where the water splashed.

That was when the whole stranger shit went away because John Watson would get all up in the queen's face if he thought something was medically wrong, so he stepped over to the man. "You're bleeding."

When the man said nothing, just continued staring at his own reflection, John turned the water off and John took his hand.

Living skin against living skin…

Sherlock took a deep breath, sighed it out as he watched Dr. John Watson of St. Mary's hospital—the introduction had come in a rush, just before the words "I'm going to touch you now"—cup his wrist in one hand, and with the other run the pad of his fingers around the butterfly plasters marching in a jagged line from Sherlock's wrist and into his upturned cuff.

The doctor moved slow, as if with his skin he could read skin, and of course that was what he was doing, sensitive fingers feeling for the heat of infection, the tight tenderness of septicity.

Along with perceiving those gentle touches, Sherlock's other senses stirred too, and standing close to Dr. John Watson of St. Mary's hospital, Sherlock could taste each coffee exhale and it made him wonder how many molecules it took for that, for a man to taste another man's breath.

While he breathed deep, thinking those thoughts, Sherlock listened to that breath's steady in and out, and it slowed Sherlock's too, and just about the time he started to think about the soporific comforts of nearness, Dr. John Watson looked into his eyes as he pressed at the bones of Sherlock's wrist, testing range of motion and—

—Sherlock remembered something from years back, a man bending his own hand, Sherlock had found it curious how far the man's wrist went—double jointed?—and while Dr. John Watson looked into his eyes to search for the tells of pain, Sherlock had a bright idea.

He expressed this by sucking in a deep, eureka-type breath. Dr. John Watson froze. Then together they spoke.

"I'm sorry I want to help where did it hurt?"

"Could a grown man have retained all his baby bones?"

Over the years John and Sherlock will tell strangers a half dozen different stories about the night they met, but there's only one they laugh and tell each other.

That was you, the very essence of who you are.

Right there is when I tumbled down your rabbit hole.

Probably they knew already, standing in the men's loo, skin on skin, molecules sneaking into each other's lungs and belly and blood, but what they did was start talking again, one over the other.

"What did you just say?"

"My wrist is fine."

"Excuse me?"

"My question?"

"Your wrist?"

"The man."

"It's not."

"What?"

They both shut up. Then opened their mouths again.

Only this time Dr. John Watson did something he would not ordinarily do when clutching a badly-doctored wrist, no, something he would not do even for the queen.

John closed his mouth.

Sherlock, reading the tells that told him of this rare largesse, took a deep breath and on the exhale said, "Infants have nearly three hundred bones, adults just over two hundred, I saw a toddler fall down a flight of stairs once, too startled to cry she just kissed her stuffed bear better and got up, seemingly no worse for wear, I wonder if having so many tiny extra bones meant her body could curve, a sort of human ball, what if an adult kept all those extra bones, couldn't he maybe bend himself, kind of fold?"

John has doctored in tattered tents, behind dusty trucks, at the top of a double-decker bus. He's tended the titled and the tiny, men, women and children of every station, at ease and in extremis. These experiences have taught the good doctor how to get the thing he wants most from a patient.

Compliance.

"I will answer that question in detail."

Sherlock huffed in anticipation and do not tell John that breath didn't smell of excitement because you will be wrong, oh yes you will.

"If you come across to St. Mary's so I can properly patch up this absurd excuse for wound care and who used butterfly plasters on you instead of stitches?"

Later Sherlock would admit he'd tended his own wound. Later still he'd learn it was to be the last one he'd ever touch, for Dr. John Watson of St. Mary's hospital would not one time ever again allow him to lay hands upon his own hurts, no, not even for a hangnail.

Unaware of this future, Sherlock nodded.

"Well," said John, "it seems those baby bones would grow with the man, making him *less* flexible. Like too many teeth crowding one against the other until none of them can move. Now, there's a rare condition called cleidocranial dysostosis, one sign of which is hypoplastic clavicles, meaning a person's shoulders can actually meet in the front. Someone with this condition may have an open fontanelle, too, allowing their skull to kind of bend."

Sherlock thinks where Sherlock will. This time it was there, leaning close to a luminous stranger and squinting at his brightness. Then suddenly, just like that, Sherlock knew where and what, how and who.

He hooted giddy, tugged at John's sleeve. "Let's go to St. Mary's hospital Dr. John Watson, and I'll let you attend to my wound. Then I'll tell you the tale of the beryl coronet in the cardboard box, of a secret inheritance and a prodigal daughter everyone, oh just *everyone,* is going to wish had never come home."

Do not argue with the good doctor when he tells you that it was then, right there that was when he smelt something rare,

221

fantastic and more than a little addictive on this tall stranger's breath.

Adventure.

They did it again, just then, John and Sherlock, they spoke at the same time and this time they said the same thing.

"Let's go."

*

When journalists ask the boys of Baker Street how they met, they usually make something up.

In a graveyard Sherlock will say, just as John replies *at the top of the BT tower.*

Once in a very great while though, they answer soft and true.

"We met in a small cafe one night," Sherlock Holmes says, "not far from Paddington Station."

And sometimes, only very rarely sometimes, John Watson adds, "It was love at first sight."

Acknowledgements

My friend Isabelle read every story in this book. She picked up each one as if it were a literary Petri dish, brought it close, peered at it and said, *"What is this? Is it supposed to be green? Why is it on fire?"*

Which is my ridiculous way of saying she helped me improve every story in this book with detailed questions and suggestions, and always with a patience and thoroughness that maybe a little bit made me want to set my hair on fire.

Which is my ridiculous way of saying thank you Isabelle, you are a pearl of rare price and I am ever grateful.

I'm also grateful to the people and places which inspired these stories, including...

Time Immemorial came from my fascination regarding the standardisation of time, something that became necessary when the telegraph began to spread. It was also prompted by my desire to write these men as boys. When my friend Lauren said, "The air is buzzing with the anticipation of years," I knew how the story ended. Thank you Lauren.

The Art of Gay Wooing, By Sherlock Holmes was the title given to me on a silver platter by Isabelle. No matter in which time, place, or canon you see John Watson and Sherlock Holmes, I think it's safe to say that if the Great Detective was ever going to woo, the manner of his wooing would not be precisely regular.

Playing Doctor was inspired by a Cumberbatch-Of-Cookies, the doctors who shared their foundation year experiences on the British Medical Journal careers website, and my imagination. Stuff I made up: The hospital at which John works. Stuff I didn't: There really are tunnels beneath Camden. How could Sherlock *not* fall in love with a man who brings him catacombs?

Sweet Talk was inspired when Dimitra suggested that the boys bicker over the last of a coveted sweet at a bakery. That the sweet was an almond croissant is completely in honour of BlackMorgan, the kindest pirate I'm privileged to know.

The Empty House. The house in this story is modeled, with artistic licence, on the glorious row of homes called St. Paul's Studios, on Talgarth Road, in London. These flats, built for "gentlemen artists," did not suffer in the war, though two bombs did fall nearby during the Blitz. Thank you Narrelle Harris for suggesting the story take place during the Blitz, and Valerie Schreiner for the ideal title.

Flipping the Switch. The HOLMES computer software is real and is currently used by the police force in the UK to help investigate serious crime. Watson is also real. An artificial intelligence software created by IBM, Watson's greatest fame has come as a winning contestant on the television game show *Jeopardy*. As for Moriarty, Adler, Trevor and Dr. Doyle, well I'm not sure, but I think they're fictional…

Because He's a Lady was one thousand percent inspired by Narrelle Harris, who has brilliant ideas and Sherlock in Victorian dress, danger money, and an iffy cabbie are just a few of them. I owe you a pretty pair of lace up boots Narrelle. I owe you lots of things.

A Crying Shame was inspired by a friend who I hope now knows that no matter how strong we are, no matter who needs our strength, there is no weakness in asking for help when we ourselves need it. When the pain is so great there are tears or cutting or thoughts of worse, we must *ask for help.*

This brings me to a short note about where the royalties for this book will go: The *It Gets Better Project.*

Profits made on *The Night They Met* will go to benefit *It Gets Better* because all of us—but especially young people like the teenagers the Project helps—can sometimes forget that *it gets better.*

Pain is not permanent, and nothing stays the same forever. After a forest burns, new things sprout, strong things.

It gets better.

It always does.

We just need the patience to wait.

SOON FROM *IMPROBABLE PRESS*

The Six Secret Loves of Sherlock Holmes

by Atlin Merrick

"Mr. Holmes, have you ever been in love?"

Detective inspector Wanda Payne stood at the head of the Scotland Yard conference table and blinked politely at the perennial burr in her side.

He blinked back at her.

When Sherlock Holmes was seven-years-old he was recognised as a genius.

At nine he was performing chemistry experiments whose formula most university students can neither write nor understand.

When Sherlock was fourteen he learned how little people like the exceptional.

At fifteen he decided he did not care.

Today, at just a bit over forty, the good detective was belatedly learning that exceptional has many sides and some are gifts, like a brain that moves fast as fire when in pursuit of clues, like tongue and fingers, nose and ears that taste touch smell hear the things his eyes do not see.

Yet along with these there's the curse of expecting from exceptional people—yourself and others—exceptional things: Honour, truth, clarity. Not the playground politics of one-upmanship, trickery, or out-right lies.

Detective inspector Wanda Payne, who long ago learned to best rivals with her words because she was too weak to best them any other way, clasped her hands behind her back. She walked slowly around the conference table, behind every one of the twelve Met detectives gathered there and again the DI said, quite courteous, "Have you, Mr. Holmes? Have you ever been in love?"

Sherlock stared at the detective for a long time. So long it could be counted—lub-dub, lub-dub—by a dozen beats of his heart.

And here's a fact: Fascination can be felt. It's a flutter of lashes as gazes shift from a consulting detective, the only one in the world, to a seat across the table from him. It can be tasted in the piquancy of murmurs, smelt in the waft of cologne and perfume as the bold shift in their seats, turning curious gazes toward a quiet man, a familiar man, for where there is Sherlock Holmes, John Watson will always be.

Along with the rest of the men and women in that bare, white room Sherlock looked at that familiar man. Sherlock looked at John Watson, his partner, his biographer, his friend, the love of his life.

Then Sherlock answered the question put to him.

"No, detective inspector Payne, I have not."

SOON FROM *IMPROBABLE PRESS*

The Adventure of the Colonial Boy

by Narrelle Harris

Watson rose with one fist clenched around the quartz, the other into a fist. "There are a good many things you don't know about me, Holmes. Even if I were an open book to you and your *amazing powers of observation*, you have not been here to *observe* me these three years. Do not presume to *know my secrets*."

"And here we are again. I have explained my absence. I have apologised for it. I had not taken you for such an unforgiving fellow, but so be it. I have sinned outrageously and must pay for it with your ill temper." Once more, the light-hearted tone carried acid in it.

Watson's mouth was set hard with fury. "Do not take that tone with me, Holmes. You led me to believe you had *died*. You sent me away on that path and I returned to find only a letter telling me you had expected to meet your death. And it is revealed that you watched me *weep* for you on that cursed path, with not a care for me – only some excuse that the cruel pretence was necessary for my safety."

Holmes was bristling, too. "I left you to your wife and your practice. You hardly had need of *me* in London. You had everything a man could wish for.'

'I mourned for you!' snarled Watson, 'For three years, I have mourned for the man I loved and I..."

229

He was struck suddenly dumb by his own unguarded words.

And then he scowled, because they were spoken now, with none to hear but the man who did not care, and they didn't matter anymore. None of it could possibly matter anymore, for he was a man without hope.

"You died," he said, still angry, still heartbroken, "And took half my soul with you, and it was all for nothing. All that grieving I did, *for nothing*."

Holmes was not softened. Watson had never thought he would be, though the words Holmes spoke next were a different kind of blow.

"Yes, you *loved* me," sneered Holmes, "Against your will. You didn't *want* to. Did you think I couldn't deduce your desire for me? Or how hard you fought against it? Why, when it seemed you would finally declare yourself, you took such fright that you pursued the first woman you saw who seemed likely to have you, and *married her*."

"And I was right to," Watson shouted, his voice thick, "You are repulsed. Disgusted by my feelings."

"As ever, Doctor Watson, you see nothing and observe less."

SOON FROM *IMPROBABLE PRESS*

All The Difference

by Verity Burns

In a small guesthouse just outside of London, one of the residents is discovered shot dead in his bed on the morning of New Year's Day.

With a finite suspect pool, and under pressure to find a fast resolution, Lestrade resorts to rather drastic measures.

He seeks out a man predictable only in his genius...Sherlock Holmes.

Returning to the scene with his genius in tow, Lestrade is greeted by the news that the case is solved.

Finger prints on the murder weapon lead back to one of the residents, and also prove that he is registered under a false name.

Records show that there is no such person as 'James Wilmington'. The prime suspect's real name is...John Watson.

Sherlock Holmes and John Watson: The Day They Met

Sherlock Holmes blinked wide-eyed at his second batch of coffees. After a moment he removed them from the silver tray, lining each on the table one beside the other. He did this so quickly his hand blurred. After a fussy few moments tidying his little coffee contingent, Sherlock dropped a fat, messy folder onto the table in front of him. He blinked quickly at bits of A4 sticking out, then  poked them back in with a twitchy finger. He nodded, pulled a crumpled, logo-emblazoned napkin out of his pocket, and smoothed it on top of the folder. Plucking a pen from behind his ear Sherlock Holmes proceeded to take his first sip of coffee.

At that initial swallow he closed his eyes. At the second sip he drew his brows. The third he bowed his head over the coffee and deeply inhaled the steam. At the fourth he jumped a few inches when a voice piped up next to him.

"You must really like coffee."

Sherlock blinked at the smiling man at the table beside his. The man was strongly-built, shorter than he, and by his slightly swollen thumb and the twitch of his left eye it was clear he was also a doctor, had a toothache, and had spent the morning giving booster jabs to unhappy children.

"IT'S FOR AN EXPERIMENT."

John Watson's eyes flew wide. Though the man at the next table over was not quite one body length away, he shouted as if he was on the other side of a cricket pitch.

"I'M FINDING THIS EXPERIMENT MUCH EASIER THAN SMOKING ONE HUNDRED AND FORTY TYPES OF TOBACCO."

"What?"

Sherlock shook his head so fast John was pretty sure he heard the man's spine subluxate.

"IT'S FOR FUTURE CASES ACTUALLY. YOU'D BE SURPRISED HOW OFTEN YOU FIND A DISCARDED CUP OF COFFEE AT A CRIME SCENE."

John and Sherlock blinked at one another. Sherlock got an idea.

"I HAVE AN IDEA." Sherlock picked up a still-steaming paper cup. "I THINK I'M A LITTLE OVER-CAFFEINATED—am I shouting?—I COULD USE SOME HELP."

John had one hour and fifty-two minutes until he had to get a root canal. It was either sit out back of this cafe and nervously await his doom, or help a hyper-caffeinated stranger do something concerning coffee.

"Sure."

"The Day They Met" is available in paperback and e-book from MX Publishing, and all online booksellers.

You can find Atlin Merrick at atlinmerrick.tumblr.com, archiveofourown.org/users/AtlinMerrick/works, and twitter.com/AtlinMerrick.